DEATH IN THE MOUNTAIN

John Hunter

GUNSMOKE

This hardback edition 2010
by BBC Audiobooks Ltd
by arrangement with
Golden West Literary Agency

ISBN 978 1 408 46293 5

British Library Cataloguing in Publication Data available.

Printed and bound in Great Britain by
CPI Antony Rowe, Chippenham and Eastbourne

Chapter One

The Virginia and Truckee was more mountain goat than railroad. In the twenty-one miles between the desert sink at Carson City and the town at the end of rail it climbed sixteen hundred feet in a series of curves which, added together, made up seventeen complete circles. Much of the time it didn't even stay on the ground. To Ken Murdock it appeared to fly. His hair rose every time it leaped off into space and rattled across a trestle that spanned one of the many canyons falling away emptily below him.

He could not see the trestles. And what he could see of the naked slopes of Mt. Davison was less than comforting, as bleak as his own face, as cold as the ice ball he carried inside him. He was not a mining man. He was a rancher from the green and fertile Klamath country of southern Oregon—had been a rancher—and comparison overwhelmed him with the stark ugliness of this terrain. There was only one thing he wanted of this place, of the town toward which he rode.

Virginia City was a mining town, stretching across the shallow valley high on the mountainside. Under it ran the vast pockets of the Comstock Lode, the greatest concentration of silver ever found. For seventeen years Virginia and its neighbors Gold Hill and Silver City had been the country's mining capital, the torrent of silver gutted from the plunging shafts flooding over the Sierra Nevada into the pockets of San Francisco owners and bankers, transforming the struggling community on the bay into the Queen City of the West. It had no lure for Ken Murdock.

The land had grown increasingly worse as he came south, especially since he had changed trains. He had had to trans-

1

fer to this local at the old crossing of the Truckee that was now renamed for General Reno, where it made its connection with the Central Pacific, and there was only one bright spot to the whole trip.

It was his first train ride and at the Reno station he had looked over the confusing rush of passengers with open curiosity. There were all kinds, drummers from the East or San Francisco traveling to call on the thriving merchants of the Washoe district, stockbrokers from California—what the people here called "over the hill"—several men in uniform heading toward the fort below the mountain—and the girl.

Ken Murdock thought of her only as the girl. He had no idea who she was or why she was taking the train for Virginia City. He had spotted her immediately when the train from the East pulled in and the trainman shepherded her down the steps. She had paused at the bottom, looking up and down the platform, and for a minute her eyes had met his fully. They were gray and the hair beneath the severe traveling bonnet had a golden red tint. She wore a dress of glove silk, gray to match her eyes. Her cheeks were full, rounded. Her lips showed red and when she spoke to the trainman her teeth flashed white. She had held his eyes for the minute, then lowered hers and followed the trainman who carried her two bags into the local.

There was only the single passenger coach at the head of a dozen express and freight cars, all pulled by the little bell-stacked engine. Ken had followed the girl into the coach, had hoped to find a seat close behind her. She was fun to watch, gave him a sense of excitement. But those seats were already filled. The place beside her was empty but he was too shy to take that. He had to go on down to the center of the car.

He divided his time between watching her, watching the barren mountainside, and thinking of his brother and the ranch they had lost.

There was no use cursing Ed. But those cattle were all they had had to show for five years of hard work. It had taken that long to build the spread, starting as they had with a few hundred head, borrowing money from the bank to fence, to put in the necessary irrigation ditch.

He sighed. He had been on his own since he was fifteen, with a brother three years his junior to raise. He thought of

2

the long, weary hours they had put in, of the depressed cattle market in the northwest that had made them decide on a trail drive south. Now all of it, everything he had achieved, was wiped out by Ed's foolishness. He was going to try to get it back.

And so, with the last little money he had salvaged, he was going to Virginia City. He was twenty-two years old. He had never before been out of southern Oregon. He had no plan. He did not know what he could do but . . .

The laboring engine went around another sharp curve. It almost threw him into the aisle and the jar brought him back to the present. The girl had swayed but caught her balance. He could tell by the angle of the bonnet above the red plush seat back that she was still looking out of the window.

The salesman in front of him stood up. Ken thought of him as a salesman because of the sample cases he had brought aboard. He walked down the car toward the water cooler at the end, staggering more than the rock of the train warranted. Ken knew the man had been drinking, had seen him lift a pint bottle a good many times. He watched him swallow the cup of water and start his return, steadying himself by catching at one seat back and then the next. Opposite the girl a lurch of the car threw him toward her. Instinctively the girl threw out a small hand to keep him from tumbling into her lap.

The salesman seized the hand, ogled down at her, a grin spreading across his loose face. Then he dropped his bulk into the seat at her side.

Ken Murdock saw him stretch one beefy arm over the plush back rest. Ken stood up. An instinctive reaction. He found himself in the aisle and stopped, feeling foolish.

Maybe they knew each other. Maybe the girl would resent him butting in. Maybe—but he had to make some move. Other passengers were looking at him. He followed the salesman to the water cooler, drank, then headed for his place.

The girl sat stiffly, turned toward the window, putting her back to the salesman. As Ken came up, the man dropped his arm, put his pudgy hand on her shoulder, shaking it lightly.

"Come on, girlie, it won't hurt to talk to Ben Huitt. I'm a respectable citizen. Yes siree. I work for Stylish Corsets and I know what women like." His laugh, though low, was high-pitched, lewd.

"Please." Her voice had a rich, carrying quality. "Go away. Just leave me alone."

"Ah, girlie . . ."

The sentence was not finished. Ken Murdock fastened his fingers in the collar of the man's coat and lifted him clear off the seat.

The salesman stood a good two inches over six feet, bigger than Murdock and twenty pounds heavier. Surprise held him befuddled, gasping.

Murdock said, "Go on back and sit down where you were."

"Now wait a minute, sonny."

Murdock's words were level, carrying promise. "I mean it."

The big man's fists clenched at his sides, then his puffed eyes ran over Murdock, over the worn shirt, clean but faded from many washings, the hickory pants, the boots, scuffed, their heels somewhat run over. But it was the gun belt on which his attention centered, the heavy revolver sagging in the worn holster. Without a word he shook free, brushed by Murdock, stumped up the aisle, sank into his seat, picked up the whiskey bottle and emptied it.

Everyone in the car had watched. Murdock felt naked under the general gawking, felt the hot flush redden his deep tan. He took off his hat.

"Sorry, ma'am, I didn't mean to put on a show." He took a step away but her gesture and word stopped him.

"Wait . . ."

He stood uncertainly.

"Sit down, please. He might come back."

Ken Murdock did not think the salesman would. He had seen men back down before. Southern Oregon was a rough country of rough and restless men. Even as a boy he had had to fight for what was his. But he took the seat, sat awkwardly, not looking at her, clutching his hat between his knees.

She studied him with a confident poise, the sun-darkened face that intensified the deep blue of his steady eyes, the dark hair with the soft curl holding it in place. His face was a little narrow for handsomeness, his cheeks thin, indrawn as if he

4

had missed too many meals. His cheekbones were high enough to suggest an Indian cast. There was a story in the family that one grandmother was half Indian. Ken had never given it much thought. He did not really care. Her words made him start.

"Thank you for getting rid of that pest."

He shrugged one shoulder. "He'd been drinking."

"I know. He smelled like a distillery. He's probably a good father and kind to his wife when he's home. But he's like a lot of men, has to prove something with women when he travels."

"I guess so." Ken had done no traveling except on a horse and within his own perimeter, and so far he had been too busy to pay any attention to women. He retreated into uneasy silence.

"What's a cowboy going to Virginia for? To shoot up the town?"

He started to protest, looked at her, then saw that she was teasing him and grinned sheepishly. He liked the way her eyes lighted. He decided to tease back. There was no ring on her ungloved hand.

"What's a young single lady going for? To find a husband?"

She sat back and laughed. "Fair enough. No, I live there. I work there."

He shot another glance at her hands. They were soft, unmarked by labor.

"You—? What kind of work?"

There was mischief in her grin. "I'm a stockbroker."

He looked bewildered enough to satisfy her and she laughed again.

"It's obvious you're not acquainted with Virginia, or for that matter San Francisco. Everybody here and over the hill trades in Comstock stocks. My uncle and I act as agents, we buy and sell shares on commission."

"Like cattle buyers?"

"Something like that."

"But—that's a man's job." He cut himself short, stumbled over an apology for the rudeness.

"You weren't." She was still smiling. "Don't be embar-

5

rassed. My uncle almost had a fit. My father died and I took over his share of the business. I'm the first female stockbroker on the Comstock and the first woman member of the Stock Exchange. But you'd be surprised how many of us buy and sell in the market, and most of the girls trust me more than they do a man."

He fumbled, flushed again, then took his chance. "Would you happen to know anything about stock in a Mr. Sutro's tunnel? If it's worth anything up here?"

The worry in his eyes gave her her cue. "Pennies on the dollar, if you can find a buyer at all. How did a cowboy happen to buy that?"

"I didn't buy it. I—" The explanation would be too long, too involved for him to attempt with the girl. Then on impulse he dug the letter out of his pocket and held it toward her. "Here . . ."

It was a personal scrawl, not a business communication, hard to decipher. She frowned over the words.

Dear Ken:
I'm sorry to have to write this to you but the truth is I have no choice. I sold the herd for nine thousand dollars which I thought was a very good price. And then I thought I saw an opportunity to make a lot of money for both of us.

They are building a tunnel here, back into the mountain. It is supposed to have two uses, to drain the mines which are very wet, and to haul out the ore to mills down along the Carson River.

A man named Sutro is behind the project. I heard him make a speech to a meeting of miners at the local Opera House and was very impressed. The tunnel has been under construction for ten years and is nearly completed. In fact it is about ready to be connected to one of the mines, the Savage, and as soon as the contract for draining it is signed and the said drainage ditch is dug in the tunnel floor, the stock should rise plenty in value.

Unfortunately, the mineowners have been fighting the tunnel project. This I did not realize when I purchased the shares. And until those mineowners sign the contracts the stock seems to have very little market. I am

6

therefore sending the shares to you and will go to San Francisco where I trust I can find employment.

Your brother
Ed.

She passed the letter back, no longer smiling. "Well— you've got a lot of company. About a hundred thousand others. You'd better mark that nine thousand down to education and go on from there."

He had forgotten his shyness now in the urgency of his problem. He shook his head doggedly.

"I can't do that. I've got to get that money back. I owe it to the bank back home. I borrowed it on the herd. I tried to give them the stock but they just laughed. They took the ranch. That's all we had."

"Didn't your brother understand what could happen?"

"He's just a kid. I shouldn't have sent him on the trail drive alone, but at our roundup a steer shoved me into a fence and broke my leg. I couldn't ride then."

"I'm sorry. I'm afraid you're not going to find it easy to recover your money. Sutro's stock is worth about as much as wallpaper. Some of the miners have used it for just that, pasted it over the cracks to keep the Washoe Zephyr out of their shacks."

He sat thinking, looking past her, out of the window. The scene there added to his depression. He had a view of a mill above them, its stacks spouting dense smoke, its spreading dump the center of a bare, lifeless waste. Hardly a tree remained on the steep slopes. What vegetation had not been cut down to feed the fires of furnace and boiler had been poisoned by the fumes from the belching stacks.

"Are you trying to say he's a crook?"

"A lot of people have called him that. Even some who used to be his friends."

"And the tunnel is never going to be used?"

"It won't if the mineowners have their way. We haven't been able to sell a share in months. But if you want to bring your shares to our office—it's on C street three doors below the Western Union office—I'll try to get a bid. I might be able to get you a few cents on the dollar."

There was a stubbornness in him that had carried him through the hard years. He shook his head slowly.

"I'll talk to this Sutro first. A few cents won't get my ranch back."

He was interrupted as the trainman pulled open the door to the car platform, shouting, "Virginia. Virginia City. The wildest, shootingest, riproaringest town in the whole United States."

The girl was adjusting her bonnet. "Well, I wish you luck Mr . . ."

"Murdock. Ken Murdock."

"And thank you again. I'm Helen Powell. Our office is Powell Brothers. If you change your mind, let me see what I can do."

He took her bags, went back for his bedroll, then followed the off-loading crowd. The girl stood at one side on the platform as he came down the steps, a short, heavy-set man limping toward her. One leg was a trifle shorter than the other and he helped his walk with a gold-headed cane. He had a round, florid face and iron-gray hair beneath an elegant beaver.

"Helen." The man planted a kiss on her cheek without removing his hat. Murdock expected it to fall off. It did not. Then he was shaking hands with the man as Helen Powell introduced them.

"My uncle, Henry Powell." She turned her head. "Mr. Murdock was very helpful to me. I would like to repay him by being of assistance, but for the life of me I don't know how. He's looking for someone to buy some tunnel shares."

Henry Powell lifted shaggy eyebrows and puffed his pink cheeks.

"Tunnel shares indeed? I doubt you could find anyone to give five cents for them. I'm sorry."

He turned away, leading his niece toward their carriage, trailed by the colored coachman carrying her bags. As the rig swung to make its way up C street the girl looked back and raised one hand in friendly salute.

Ken Murdock lifted his wide, worn hat and watched her go. Then he was very much alone in the strangest town he had ever seen.

8

Chapter Two

The Crystal Palace Saloon was the most elaborate of the hundred bars that catered to the citizenry. The floors above the barroom were given over to the Washoe Club, the most exclusive brotherhood of mineowners, superintendents, leading merchants and legislators that the new state boasted. But on the ground floor the Crystal, like all of Virginia's saloons, was open to anyone. The miner just off shift, still in his dirt-stained clothes, received as prompt and courteous service as any of the silver kings.

Ken Murdock came into the big room at nine o'clock of his first night in Washoe. He had found a modest boarding house on B Street, had an early supper, then walked from one end of the surging town to the other, pausing to stare in the windows of the many stores, fascinated by the new and totally unexpected riches they displayed.

No store in Virginia closed before midnight. No bar ever closed. The mines worked three shifts and there were always fresh customers with thirsts to quench.

Ken pushed open the louvered doors of the Crystal and stopped, gaping. He had never seen its like, the glittering overhead chandeliers, their sparkling prisms reflected in the great, ornate mirrors, the tiers of gleaming glassware stacked and ready for instant use along the long mahogany backbar.

There were at least two hundred men lined against the polished counter. Six bartenders in white coats worked in a frantic rhythm. Every table in sight was filled. The noise, the laughter wrapped him in a smothering blanket. He stood undecided for a full minute, then moved forward carefully and edged in to the bar between two groups of boisterous men.

No one noticed him. He waited patiently until one bartender stopped in his hurry and asked his pleasure. He ordered whiskey, had a small glass and a bottle set before him immediately. Then the man was gone.

He poured his drink, drank it slowly, his eyes on the backbar mirror, studying the room. The bartender came past a second time and Ken motioned to him.

"They told me I'd probably find a Mister Sheldon here. He's with the tunnel company."

The bartender, poised for flight, raked his eyes along the row of drinking men. He shook his head. "Don't see him. He's usually here about this time. You might try the Magpie."

"Where's that?"

"Two blocks down, beyond the International Hotel."

Ken Murdock paid for his drink and worked crabwise through the crowd, dodging a group of miners just coming in through the wide doorway. On the street he paused for a quiet breath. Winter was strong in the air. The wind sweeping up from the Devil's Gate was cold, raw, beating. He snuggled his chin deep into the collar of his sheep-lined coat and pushed down the jammed sidewalk, making little better time than the traffic in the rutted street. It too was filled, with a continuous line of ore carts, supply wagons, and the spanking buggies and carriages of the richer citizens.

The men he passed were a broadly international lot. Virginia was a lodestone, a melting pot for every color and every tongue. Irish, German, Cornish and Welshmen from the coal mines of their distant native land, come to the new world to wrench the treasure from the stark Nevada earth. Here were Negroes recently freed, Chinese, Indians, lithe and smiling men from the Sandwich Islands, mingling with native-born Americans who had shoved West from the eastern seaboard and midwest farms.

If a man could work, would work, Virginia had a place for him.

The Magpie was not as flamboyant as the Crystal, but it was warm and comfortable after the biting mountain wind. Ken loosened his coat and worked toward the bar. The smell of cinnamon and nutmeg from the big punchbowl there added a pungency to the tobacco-heavy air. The punch was free to any who wanted it, rum-loaded, potent, creamy.

Ken Murdock passed up the punchbowl. He found a place

between a reeking miner and a tall man in a high hat and a waistcoat decorated with a horse design that was worked in gold thread; a gambler, Ken judged.

He ordered his drink and again stood studying the reflection in the mirror. This room was as crowded as the Palace but without its show of richness. Here there were no chandeliers, but wall lamps, light from the small gas flames thrown outward by polished reflectors. Still, a dozen poker games flourished at the rear, a roulette layout and a faro bank stood side by side along the opposite wall, both hemmed in by a silent crowd that jostled each other in good temper to get down their bets.

There were two bartenders. One was short and heavy, his stomach swelling under a spotted apron. The second was taller with stooped shoulders and a mask of a face, expressionless with his concentration.

Murdock waited until the short man filled his second drink, then asked his question.

"Is Mr. Sheldon here? The one with the tunnel company?"

The bartender looked up from the glass. The gambler half turned, measured Ken thoughtfully. The bartender jerked a thumb.

"The man at the back table. The one with the slouch hat."

Murdock looked down the room. Sheldon was stocky but had a keen, perceptive face. He was talking with a man across the table. They seemed to be arguing. Murdock stayed where he was until the second man rose and left, then he shifted through the crowd to Sheldon's chair.

Ken Murdock stood above the man, silent, until his presence forced Sheldon's eyes up to meet his. The tunnel man's face was still dark from the argument, the eyes bitter and brooding. The gaze came up slowly, taking in the cowhand clothes, recognizing that this was no miner, no resident of the mountain.

"Well?" The tone was short with a residue of an earlier anger. "What do you want? A job?"

"No, Mr. Assistant Superintendent." Murdock lowered himself unasked into the opposite seat. "What I want is nine thousand dollars."

Sheldon blinked. It took him a moment to force his mind

11

away from the interview he had just been through, to focus on this stranger before him.

"The hell you say. Who doesn't? Why come to me?"

Once again Ken Murdock dug out his brother's letter and spread it on the table. His voice was tight, controlled.

"Read that."

Sheldon skimmed through it and flipped the sheet back, shrugging. "So hold onto the shares until the price comes up."

The frustration that had been building in Murdock boiled close to the surface but he held his temper. He had to convince this man. He leaned forward now in desperate tension.

"Listen to me, Mr. Sheldon. I spent five years of hard work building that herd, and almost all of the price it brought I owed to the bank. It wasn't Ed's to spend. Now the bank's taken my ranch. I want it back. And if your company is any kind of an honest outfit you'll buy this stock in for what Ed paid for it."

Sheldon's mouth dropped open in pure astonishment. He had a welling up of almost uncontrollable laughter, but he cut it off, looking into the earnest eyes, reading the wild temper so close behind them.

He felt that he was on the ragged edge of explosion himself. After all of the years of following Sutro's dream, bulling through, surviving every catastrophic setback, harried and harrassed and thwarted at every turn, in these last days he had thought he saw daylight ahead. He had thought the great work would soon be finished and justified, and then to have the damned Savage mine superintendent back out, refuse to honor the last agreement—there was more pressure bottled up within him than he could tolerate. Now this young pious bumpkin prattling at him about his picayune loss—with the stupid gall to call Adolph Sutro a crook. He was going to burst.

He must not. That would be the end. This boy was wearing a gun and he was hot enough to use it.

He swallowed, crowded down the yell for the idiot to clear out, forced his voice to a stringent level.

"Adolph Sutro is an honest man. A big, big man. He is fighting with his life for a concept that must be realized. That *must* be. I have not been paid for weeks. Most of the officers haven't been paid. But we're hanging on. Why? Because we believe. In Adolph Sutro. In the tunnel. I couldn't buy your shares if I wanted to. So you've lost a ranch. So you don't like bankers ..."

Murdock cut in. "I didn't say that. I owed them the money. I pay my debts ..."

"Shut up and listen," said Sheldon. "I don't like them either. And God knows Sutro has reason not to. They're the reason the tunnel isn't finished, being used, making money. If it were, your stock would be worth a hundred times what you paid for it." He bent forward suddenly and beat a fist on the table. "And it's going to be finished. You just put that under your hat. It has to be finished."

He felt a strange edge of relief, as if the small outburst had let a wisp of cool air slip into the steam that filled his head. Partly it was the startled, open look with which the stranger sat back, but more, it was his own words, the thoughts that prudence had taught him he must not say aloud on this mountain. It was like a taste of water in the desert. It demanded more. And yet it was so dangerous. He tried to back off, caught the eye of a waiter and signaled for a second glass, filled it and poured his own drink from the bottle already on the table, shoved the one across and tossed the other down his throat.

It did not work. The man facing him ignored the drink, asked a question.

"What's so important about that tunnel? You're pretty steamed up about it."

Against all of his judgment, Sheldon went on. "It's important because it's so desperately needed. There have been horrible fires in the mines, hundreds of men killed. And all the lower levels are full of poison gasses. The air down there is so hot the miners can only work a few minutes at a time. The sumps are full of boiling water that scalds everything it touches. Only Sutro's tunnel can sufficiently ventilate the shafts. Only the tunnel can drain off the hot water. Only the tunnel makes a way of escape for men when they're trapped by underground fire. Ask the miners what it means, the men who came up with their little dabs of money in spite of the banks. You think you've lost something. If they lose that tunnel . . ."

Ken Murdock did not hide his confusion, his skepticism, saying, "But if all that's so, why don't the people who own the mines put the tunnel in?"

"Blind greed. They don't give a damn about the men. All they care about is profits, dividends. We've had to battle them as well as the banks all the way."

Sheldon stopped again, filled his glass and drank. The other man had not touched his whiskey. Sheldon was too intent on himself to care why. The relief of talking was physical, like a draining infection. Maybe it was the liquor that lessened his caution, but it should be all right with this audience, an out-of-towner not involved with any faction of the fight. He relaxed against the chair back, even felt a small smile stretch his stiff lips.

"You don't know much about what's going on here, do you?"

Ken Murdock shook his head. "I never heard of the tunnel or Sutro either until Ed's letter."

Sheldon barely let him finish. "All right, I'll tell you. Adolph Sutro visited this camp way back in 1860, before the mines were really open or the camp really started. The most unlikely man you could find to do what he's done. He was a tobacco merchant, born in Germany of Jewish stock. He wasn't an engineer at all. Just a very smart man. He saw then that they were going to need a tunnel to work the mines right, saw that it could be run four miles in through the base of the mountain and open out down by the river.

"Everybody was strong for the idea then. The federal government gave him a charter and all the men who owned the mines then and the Bank of California got behind it. The mines agreed to pay for hauling their ore out plus a royalty of two dollars a ton of their production for draining off the water. New mills were to be built down along the river.

"Then a man named Shannon came along, as representative of the Bank of California, loaning millions to the Comstock mines and mills, and when the hard times came in the middle sixties he foreclosed everything. And the bank owned almost the whole lode. But it didn't own the tunnel.

"It dawned on Shannon and his directors that it would cost

14

them a hell of a lot in royalties to use that tunnel. And from then on they threw every monkey wrench they could. They blacklisted Sutro, cut off his credit in the East. Adolph went to Europe for new backing. And he applied to Congress for a subsidy. The bank blocked him cold. Then he seemed to get a break. The bank overextended itself and had to close. A new group took control of the Comstock, four Irishmen headed by John Mackay and James Fair, slippery Jim they called him. We thought they'd see the need for the tunnel. But they didn't. They blocked us the same way the bank had—until the fire in the Savage.

"It started there and spread to other mines, the Kentucky for one. Forty-five men died in that fire, but it gave us a new lease on life. The miners' union rose up in arms. And it was they who gave Sutro the money to go on—men who knew what it was to risk their lives every day, down there with no protection . . ."

Sheldon's words that had been pouring like a torrent choked off, his eyes anchored above Murdock's head, his face tightened, whitened. His lips pressed tight.

Ken Murdock felt a prickle at the back of his neck. He recognized the coming of trouble, for Sheldon was suddenly a very frightened man. Ken did not turn. He was motionless, watching Sheldon, seeing from the sides of his eyes the five men who slowly surrounded the table, big bodies that blocked off the rest of the room.

One of them spoke in a low tone to Sheldon.

"You've been warned enough not to talk in public places. This finishes it. We're putting you on the midnight train. And you are not coming back." He lifted cold, flat eyes across the table. "Who might you be?"

Murdock's impulse was to say it was none of their business but he checked it. Sheldon's face showed him that this was not a time for useless challenge.

"Ken Murdock. Linkville, Oregon."

"What do you want with Sheldon?"

"I was talking to him about the price of some cattle."

"You've finished talking. Get out of here, cowboy, while you're still healthy."

Murdock had not the slightest idea what this was all about. He stood up slowly, able to see that every eye in the

15

room was on this table. Complete silence had fallen. Men were edging off, getting out of the possible line of fire. He looked down at Sheldon, sensing the man's deep fear, and yet there was no attitude of cringing or begging.

One of the fence of men stepped aside, gave him passage. Ken went through, walked a dozen steps, glanced back. The cold-eyed man had wrapped his hand around Sheldon's arm.

Ken went on to the bar that was vacant now. He turned deliberately, brushing back the skirt of his coat. His curved fingers lifted the gun from its holster, brought it up in a little sweeping gesture. He raised his voice to carry the distance.

"Just hold on. Just take your hands off Mr. Sheldon."

A shock wave went with the words, freezing the room, the five men at the table he had left. All of them wore guns as if they lived by them. They understood them, and by their stillness they showed that all of them believed Murdock would shoot. The cold-eyed man's head came around with extreme care.

"Keep out of this, kid. It's not your fight."

"Let go of Sheldon."

The man dropped his hand. There was fury in his voice, at having ignored this apparently harmless cowhand.

"Buster, you're in now. I won't forget."

"If you live to remember."

Ken Murdock did not know what made him say that. He had never said anything like it before. He had had his troubles, his fights, when he and Ed had started their ranch. The bigger outfits had resented them, had expected to run them out easily. Ken had not run. He had guarded his fences with his gun. He had wounded three riders before he was let alone.

But he had never before been up against hired killers, and instinct told him that all five of these were just that. Whatever the case, the big man was right. He was in it now. He called.

"All of you, drop your guns. I'm not going to say it twice."

He held his breath, watching the moment of hesitation, seeing the instant when they made up their minds. One decided to try. His knees bent for the rushing turn. He got only halfway around before Ken Murdock's bullet broke his gun arm just above the wrist.

16

The others moved not a hair.

Ken leveled his gun on the man who was spokesman for the group. His knuckle tightened against the trigger. They had waited for that proof. As one they dropped their weapons to the sawdust floor.

"Now your belts."

Slowly they let the belts slide.

"All of you, walk over against the rear wall. Face it. Put your hands on it above your heads. Lean on them."

They were sullen, lagging, but they followed the order.

As they went, Murdock threw a quick look at the bar mirror, measuring the rest of the room. No one had so much as shifted a foot. None had showed the least interest in taking a part in the play.

"Now, Mr. Sheldon, you pick up that stuff, take it out of here."

The tunnel executive had sat stunned by the unexpected action, by its swiftness. He shook himself alert, left the chair, gathered up the guns, then the belts, and headed for the door. Four of the guns bristled up from his belt. The fifth one he carried, leveled. The five belts were slung over his shoulder, their weight dragging it down so that he walked at a stoop. He covered the full length of the silent room, his footsteps measuring his progress. Ken kept his eyes on the men against the wall. Not until he heard the doors flap shut after Sheldon did he speak. His voice reached every corner of the saloon.

"Don't anybody come out to the street for five minutes. If you do, I'll be waiting."

He edged sidewise, his hip against the bar, turned so that he could watch both the gunmen and the mirror. His was the only movement. He felt the doors against his shoulders and backed through, spun quickly to one side.

Sheldon waited across the board sidewalk. He still had the guns but the belts were out of sight. Murdock's glance was question enough. Sheldon was grinning, a new bright excitement in his eyes. He jerked his head toward a trash container beneath the edge of the porch roof.

"Under some paper. Come on, boy, let's get away from here."

Chapter Three

The buggy was light, the team fresh and full of run. Sheldon weaved in and out of the thinning traffic, paying no attention to the shouts of angered teamsters. He took them over the low crest, through Gold Hill, down the narrow, tortuous grade past the Devil's Gate and Silver City. They dropped out of Gold Canyon above Dayton on the Carson River and turned northeast along the valley toward the town at the tunnel's mouth that Sutro had named for himself.

Sheldon drove fast when finally he had the room, but he handled the team like an expert. Neither of them had spoken while he fought the ore wagons and supply trains for running room, grazing more than one wheel hub as he squeezed by. Murdock used the time to reappraise this man whom he had first thought was a jittery, conniving trickster trying to fast-talk him out of even wanting to recoup his money. After the initial show of shock at the arrival of the gunmen he had appeared unafraid, even though he was obviously unarmed and at the mercy of men who plainly would kill him on their whim. That kind of courage commanded respect.

Now on the wide, straight valley road Sheldon turned for a long, close study of the man beside him, his eyes shrewd with a growing thought.

"Many, many thanks, son. You pack a surprise wallop. I didn't put you down for having the stomach to pull that kind of stunt."

Murdock said nothing. He was always embarrassed under praise. Sheldon's face crinkled into a grimace of conflicting emotions.

"Right now I wish to hell I could hand you your nine thousand dollars. I can't. I doubt there's that much in the company kitty. We're living on what Adolph and a few friends can bring in. But if you wanted to risk staying around

18

until we get our first connection made, maybe we could do something."

Sheldon's dubious tone made Murdock ask, "What risk do you mean?"

"Mainly Shaw and his bully boys. You made a dangerous enemy there tonight."

"Who are they anyway?"

"Company police. They guard the money rooms for some of the mines. They search the miners in the change rooms to keep them from walking off with ore. They ride over everybody, use fear to keep their power, and they can't afford to have their hand called. They know it and they'll try to take care of you if you stay in the country."

Ken Murdock grunted, a bitter sound. "Don't look like I could stay long anyway. Things are right expensive in Virginia."

Sheldon nodded as if something had been proven to him. "I could give you a job—could sure use you—been looking for someone like you. But with Shaw on your trail I feel like I'm asking you to commit suicide."

"Thanks for the thought, but I don't know anything about digging a tunnel."

"I wasn't thinking about digging."

Murdock turned his head to look at Sheldon. "Then what would you want me to do?"

"Fight." Sheldon bit the word off.

"How does fighting fit in? I thought this was a financial war."

Sheldon's mouth was grim. "Above ground it is. Down below there's always been fighting. For instance, one mine crew would run its drifts over into its neighbor's property and the battle was on for possession of the ore."

"Wouldn't the law stop that?"

"Law!" Sheldon barked a laugh. "Law on this mountain belongs to whoever is strongest, who has the most guns. There are more legal suits piled up now than the courts can clear up in years."

"But you're not mining. Why would the tunnel have to fight?"

"Because we're close to breaking through into the Savage,

and the Hale and Norcross. Sutro has told both managements that he could take their water as soon as our ditch is ready but he won't until they live up to their commitments—agree to pay the royalties and charges. They're threatening to dump their water on us without paying.

"We've built a bulkhead to prevent that, and I suspect they will try to tear it out. Your job would be to see that they don't. We could pay you a hundred and fifty a month."

A hundred and fifty dollars a month! During his riding days Ken Murdock had never made more than forty, and often in the winter months only twenty-five. With a salary like this he could save up a stake. When—if—Sutro and the mines made their deal, if the stock went up, if he could buy back his ranch, he should have enough to go forward without further borrowing. That was a position he had not expected to reach for years. He found the first smile he had known in weeks.

"Mr. Sheldon, you just hired yourself a man."

Sheldon drew a long, ragged breath. "I hope—I hope—" he did not say just what he hoped. There were too many hopes to choose among.

The town of Sutro was laid out in a rectangular grid. In an age when towns, especially mining camps, grew up along existing trails, spreading their shacks and then their more substantial buildings in a patternless maze, this one was an exception. Adolph Sutro had an orderly mind and he conceived his town for growth. He expected it to become the biggest community in Nevada. Why not? Once all the ore being taken from the lode was pouring through the tunnel to mills along the river for treatment and shipment, Virginia City and her sister towns on Mount Davidson would shrivel and die. The prospect was already a major worry to the businesses now fattening near the mine heads.

It was after two in the morning when Sheldon wheeled his rig through the quiet streets and pulled into the company livery, near the structure protecting the tunnel entrance.

Murdock stepped down as the night hostler came to take the team, then walked at Sheldon's side to a bunkhouse where his new boss said he should spend the night.

All of the quarters furnished for his men by Adolph Sutro were much superior to the private boarding houses used by

20

the miners of the district. Throughout his career Sutro had kept close to his employees. He took a paternal interest in all their affairs, concerned that they have decent shelter, food, medical care. His was the first operation on the Comstock to maintain a company doctor and give free periodic checkups to its workmen.

Murdock came into a small room, spartan but individual. The board and batten walls were pasted over with muslin cloth. There was a single hard bunk, a stand with washbowl and pitcher, a shelf with a row of hooks below it in lieu of a wardrobe.

Murdock did not need more. Other than the clothes he wore he possessed one change, wrapped neatly in his bedroll. Nor was the hard bunk a problem. More of his life's nights had been spent on the ground than in a bed. He spread his blanket and wrapped himself in it, but in spite of the hour sleep did not come at once. Too much was strange here. Too much new had happened to him since he had set out from his native, familiar Linkville in his desperate effort to save his ranch.

The changes crowded on him. The meeting with the girl on the train, Helen Powell, stood out distinctly from the rest and he drifted into sleep wondering if he would ever see her again.

Sounds from the rooms around him roused him too soon. The cold water from the pitcher did not fully freshen him and he noticed little as he breakfasted with a motley crowd in the common dining room. It took the walk through the brittle cold morning, to the office at the tunnel entrance, to wake him. There he reported to the superintendent, Jack Bluett.

Bluett was one of the oldest employees on the project. He had started as a laborer, earned the position of superintendent of one of the ventilating shafts driven vertically down through the mountainside, and by long perserverance had risen steadily. Now he supervised all three shifts working in the tunnel. He had a bulldog chin that perpetually jutted further forward than his broken nose, a habit developed through his years of controlling the rough, burly crews. His head snapped up as Murdock came through his door. His voice was like a hammer.

21

"Who the hell are you?"

Murdock jarred back. He had thought he would meet Sheldon here, had asked for him when he was stopped by a man outside the door, and felt at a loss that this blocky man did not expect him.

He said mildly, "Ken Murdock. Mr. Sheldon hired me last night."

Jack Bluett's raking eyes held no welcome. He pulled a paper to him across his desk, read it slowly, his lips moving as he followed the words, then he tossed it aside, grunting.

"So. A cowpoke who pulled Nanny Sheldon out of a jam uptown."

Murdock made no answer. He resented the mocking tone.

"A gunfighter, it says here." He flicked a finger at the paper.

Murdock's voice had an edge. "I have a gun, mister, and I know how to use it. But I'm not a hired killer, if that's what you mean."

Bluett sat back against his chair, chewed on a dead cigar stub. "Oh, you don't like the name gunfighter? That's what Sheldon hired you for. If you aren't a gunfighter, what are you? Drill master? Powder man? Mucker? What? I'm supposed to put you to work, it says. Doing what? Maybe you can drive a mule?"

Controlling his temper had been one of Ken Murdock's harder jobs. It flared now under this man's gratuitous insult.

"It was Mr. Sheldon's idea to hire me. I told him I'm no tunnel man. I've never been underground and I'm not just crazy about going. Sorry I bothered you."

He pivoted to stalk out. Bluett shot a word after him.

"Wait."

Murdock stopped, looked over his shoulder. Bluett was eyeing him up and down like a man buying a horse.

"You claim you can use that gun. Let's see. Just how good can you handle it? There are tough men on this mountain. Plenty of them."

Murdock felt like a fool. "To hell with you," he said and went on toward the door.

"I told you to wait. Come back here and put your feathers down."

Murdock hesitated and Bluett went on, grumbling at Ken's back.

"Nanny's a confounded idiot—always gets himself in trouble, every time he goes to Virginia. Knows good and well the mine people up there hate our guts but up he goes, has a few drinks and talks too much. So you backed down Buck Shaw."

Murdock made a slow turn. "I had the drop on him."

"Think you could meet him head on?"

"I don't know. I haven't seen him handle a gun."

Bluett's clamshell mouth spread in a sudden smile. It changed his whole face, did not soften it but somehow let the warmth of the man show through.

"Kid, I guess you're all right. My job to find out."

Murdock was still ruffled but Bluett went on, conciliatory now.

"I had to make sure of you. You aren't the first gun we've hired, probably won't be the last. There's trouble enough to go around. With the mine police, with miners going on their rampages, with our own crews. It takes a tough breed to work underground with the temperatures running up over a hundred and twenty. I didn't want some brash kid who'd throw his weight around and get himself killed the first time a miner took after him with a single jack. I need somebody with some horse sense." He stood up, beckoning with a thick arm. "Come on, I'll show you around."

Murdock still hesitated. Under the tempting thought of the big salary he had not really considered where he would be working. Born and raised as an outdoor creature he had a natural abhorrence of the dark, deep reaches of the underground world. Still, he had committed himself to Sheldon. He shucked off his sheep-lined jacket and followed Bluett.

Chapter Four

Adolph Sutro was a visionary, not a trained engineer, but also he was careful, meticulous, methodical, thorough. He had visited the Hoosac Tunnel in Massachusetts, studying it under construction. He had consulted the leading engineering authorities of Europe. He had incorporated all of the latest improvements in his specifications. The tunnel he was digging was a masterpiece, and dovetailed into his larger scheme.

Its entrance was approximately a mile back from and above the Carson River, high enough that there would never be a danger of flooding from the stream. Straight out from the entrance ran Tunnel Avenue, the main street of the company-dominated town.

Even the mansion which Sutro had built for himself over-looking the young trees that marched down the regimented streets, was part of the company operation. Sutro used it when he was in Washoe as both office and home.

The same precision of progression obtained within the tunnel. First Ken Murdock followed Bluett through the door in the portal which supported the earth around the mouth. It led them into the lamp room where rows of racks held miners' lamps and the collar lamps that were affixed to each mule as it hauled its single car. The wall lights cast grotesque shadows from the half dozen twelve-year-old boys busy filling the lamps. To Murdock it seemed a cave.

He let Bluett fit him with a cap and lamp and trailed him through another door into a dark, humid, echoing corridor where bright, narrow gauge rails glinted, and climbed into the inspection car. The car was like the body of a buggy, but with a flat wooden roof for protection from falling rock. It was mounted on cross springs to absorb some of the jolt as the patient, drooping mule pulled it down the tracks. The tracks were uneven, built of wood to save money and faced with thin iron strips over which the iron-rimmed wheels rumbled. Beside them a square, covered wooden flume snaked off ahead, as far as they could see.

They could not see far. There were bracket lights set some hundred feet apart but between those glowing pools only the lamps they carried kept the gloom from shutting down upon them.

The tunnel was roomy but even so the walls, floor, ceiling of heavy timbers pressed in on Murdock like some gigantic coffin. Bluett stopped at each of the two vent shafts drilled down from the surface, explaining the blowers that forced air into the long haulage way, the boxed-in pipes that carried air

24

to the drills being used at the face. To Murdock it was a reminder of how far beneath that surface he was getting, how much of crushing mountain rose above him. And even with the forced air a suffocating heat increased. In his shirtsleeves he was soon soaked through, not from temperature alone.

Then they were at the bulkhead and Bluett ordered the car stopped again. Here the driver climbed down, pulled a bucket that tinkled with ice water from the back of the car, took it forward and held it for the mule to drink.

Ken Murdock watched with jealous interest. He had never heard of giving an animal ice water, and at the moment he would almost have traded places. But Bluett took no drink and he was damned if he would ask.

Bluett was explaining again, his voice warm with a fondness Ken had not heard there before. The man had only two real loves. One was his loyalty to Adolph Sutro. The other was a compassion for the hundreds of mules that dragged supplies the long four miles to the face and hauled out the rock the miners had blown. Tough as they were, the little animals could not withstand the heat, and every one that died was a personal loss to the feisty superintendent.

"We use a hell of a lot of ice on the mules, and it still doesn't save them," he said. "They're wonderful animals, Murdock, and we lose one or two every day in spite of everything we can do. Be sure you never stand beside one of them. They collapse of the heat without warning, just fall over. If you're in the way they'll crush you. That's happened to three men so far.

"Climb down now and look at the bulkhead. It's important. And the mine people would love to destroy it."

The lecture was detailed and impressive. Long stretches of the tunnel were gouged out of clay seams, soft material, but here the bore had been driven through solid rock. Masonry walls of cut stone were built across it, the blocks fitted together and cemented, fifty-two inches thick. Enough, Bluett said with satisfaction, to withstand a column of water five thousand feet high. The bulkhead was built at a narrow neck so that the pressure from beyond would force the masonry into the throat and wedge it tighter and tighter.

Openings had been left for two-way traffic of the ore cars,

and doors for these openings were swung back against the bulkhead walls, doors made of solid slabs of sugar pine over thirty inches thick.

"She ought to hold it back," Bluett said grimly. "If the bastard mineowners do try to dump their stinking, boiling water down on us."

The solid fact of the thing standing there brought reality to Bluett's unreal words. Murdock caught his breath.

"Would anybody actually do a thing like that?"

"All part of the game, is the way they look at it." Bluett was bitter. "Our face is getting close to the Savage mine. We're coming in just under their sixteen-hundred-foot level, between that and their lower workings. They're draining those laterals into their sumps now, but they can pump it up and flood it in here. We can't handle that water yet, not until we get our big ditch dug and built, but the bulkhead will block it, force it back into their workings. Meanwhile the mines are playing poker with Sutro, balking at signing the contracts unless he cuts his price in half."

He pointed to a channel in the floor that carried off the seepage of the tunnel. Murdock had not noticed how far back the covered culvert had stopped.

"It's going to take time, money, work to bring the big ditch up to here. The channel has to be dug out three-feet square and lined with three-inch redwood planks, then covered tight enough so water and steam don't leak through. If the mines dump on us before that, God knows what could happen. Hot as it is it might wash the clay out from behind some supports and bring our whole works caving in. That's why this bulkhead has to be protected."

Murdock frowned in puzzlement. "I'd think you'd have guards already."

Bluett's laugh held no humor. "We do. You didn't think you were supposed to do it alone, did you?"

Murdock flushed. He had gotten that idea.

"We've got them," Bluett said, "but not one man among them who can stand up to Buck Shaw. That's where you fit. That's why I had to find out first thing if you were just a braggart kid or whether you could really do what Sheldon thought."

Murdock looked around him. There was no one else at the

bulkhead. There were men all along the tunnel, mule drivers hauling powder and freshly sharpened bits inside, hauling out cars of broken rock, hauling up square sets for the timber men to place. But no one wearing a gun.

"Where are these guards?"

"Some back at the entrance—nobody gets in here without a pass—some up ahead in case the Savage miners break through—that's where trouble will come from, the mine. You'll meet them at the face."

Bluett led the way back to the car and they drove through the bulkhead, on through an area where construction was less and less complete, where men were staking out the path of the ditch, where timbering was being strengthened. And then they were at the naked rock of the face, swallowed in a racket such as Murdock had never heard.

From the bulkhead on the noise had grown, the slam of air hammers punching holes for the afternoon's shots.

Air hammers had been familiar on the Comstock for ten years but Sutro, fighting costs, had only used them lately. Until then the tunnel had been bucked through by hand, by men with single jacks beating into the stubborn rock the star-shaped drills that their partners held and turned between blows. Now, with the air hoses and compressors, the speed of the work had tripled. They were moving forward three hundred feet a month.

Jack Bluett filled his chest and roared, and was barely heard by the foreman of the work gang. He came toward them, a walking barrel stripped to the waist, his face and body black except where rivers of sweat streaked down him like war paint. Bluett introduced him as Evans, and the hand he wrapped around Ken Murdock's fingers all but crushed them.

Unexpectedly the raw rock beneath their feet shook heavily. Murdock had to force himself to keep from running. A red grin split Evans' face.

"Don't get throwed, sport. It's just the Savage boys shooting a blast." There was still a lot of Welsh in his accent.

Murdock looked around him, at the solid rock prison. "How far away are they?"

"Hard to tell. Some formations carry the shock farther

27

than others. I'd say not much of a piece. The men don't like it."

Murdock breathed the hot air shallowly. It stung his lungs, stifled him.

"Don't like it? I'd think they'd be glad that the work in this hellhole is about finished."

"They don't mind that. It's what can happen when we hole through that bothers them. You think this air is bad, you ought to smell the lower works of the mines."

Murdock could not imagine anything worse than this sustaining life. He was dizzy, afraid he would keel over like Bluett's mules. To fight it he concentrated on what Evans was saying.

"That's the question, where will it go. Sutro says the hole we punch will act like a chimney, suck our air up through the mine. But if that's true, why don't their shaft draw up their bad air?"

Ken did not know. "Well, smoke goes up a fireplace chimney . . ."

"The men say the bad air sinks, that it will come down here and smother us all. They're scared. Some of them quit after every shift. I got a hell of a time keeping a full crew."

Murdock had no wonder at that. His own single concern was to stay alive long enough to get out of here. This was the first job he had ever felt unable to handle.

His eyes followed the driver of the buggy as he pulled a second bucket from under a tarpaulin behind the seats and set it on a shelf above his head in a space hollowed out of the wall for tool and powder storage. The bucket was beaded with moisture, filled with broken ice. Ken reeled toward it, reached up and brought out a chunk twice the size of his fist. He licked it, rubbed it over his burning face, rubbed it down his arm.

Suddenly the ice was jerked from his hand. He jumped in surprise. The mule's head was stretched forward, the ice in its teeth. Murdock snatched for it instinctively but the mule twisted its head, rolled its lips back in a threat.

Behind Murdock, laughter boomed above the air hammer. He swung around. Both Evans and Bluett were doubled up, roaring. The miners had turned from the face, grinning. Two

28

guards whom he had not met were laughing. Bluett controlled himself, gasping.

"You're lucky to have your hand, Murdock. She'd have bit it off for that ice. That's why we have to keep it up out of reach."

Murdock stared back at the black animal. The ice was gone and the head was pushing forward hopefully.

"Get away from me, you hammerheaded devil."

The mule was not impressed by the yell. It kept coming, threatening to trap him in the shallow tool shed. He jumped aside. Bluett noticed his red, dripping face.

"That's enough for the first day." He caught Murdock's arm, steered him up into the buggy.

The driver turned it onto the outgoing track and took them back through the bulkhead. The air grew noticeably cooler, fresher as they headed for the entrance. Nevertheless Bluett halted the car at the nearest blower and made Murdock stand in its draft, cool out for several minutes.

"The first day's bad, but it'll surprise you how soon you get used to it," Bluett encouraged. "Lot of men pass out their first time up at the face and we have to haul them out limp."

Murdock clenched his teeth on his answer and rode the last mile in silence, thinking hard. If he was going to quit, now was the time to do it. But when they reached the change room he still had not spoken. He tightened his lips, tossed his heavy coat over his arm and started for the outside door.

Bluett stopped him. "Put that on, it's near zero outside. In this thin air you can get pneumonia in a minute."

Murdock thought that he would never be cool again, but silently he shrugged into the coat.

"Another thing," Bluett said. "The place you stayed last night is just for new men. The police bunk together." He opened the door, called to the man with a rifle lounging outside. "Stucki, come here."

The man rolled around the jamb, a big man with a heavy face and thick-lipped mouth. His eyes were gun-metal gray and just as hard.

"This is Ken Murdock," Bluett told him. "Take him down to the boarding house. Tell the boys he's the new boss and he takes orders directly from me."

Stucki's eyes flicked with surprise and instant dislike, then he rolled back through the door, said over his shoulder, "Come on."

Murdock hesitated a moment longer, then cast his lot and followed.

They went down the slope, past the artificial lake before the office, toward the board and batten buildings grouped around the intersection of Tunnel and Adele Avenues. Stucki threw him a sidelong, mocking glance.

"So you're going to boss us, huh? You're Newcastle, mister. Where'd you learn to be a policeman?"

Ken started to admit that he knew nothing about it, but Stucki's tone stopped him and he said merely, "Oregon."

Stucki snorted and turned in at the corner building, led him into a long room where a cluster of chairs were ranged around a fat-bellied stove that glowed cherry red. After the sharp outdoor cold the room felt overwarm but there was a fragrance of wood smoke that was pleasant.

"Sheila. Hey, Sheila, I got another boarder for you."

A girl appeared in the dining-room door, small, with blue eyes heavily fringed in dark lashes. Black hair parted precisely and plaited into two thick braids that hung over her shoulders made her seem a child. But there was no childishness in the tart voice.

"I'm not deaf, you don't need to shout at me."

If she were angry, Stucki seemed not to notice. He cupped a hand under her chin and tilted the red mouth up.

"Here you are, a kiss will sweeten you up."

She batted the dirty hand away. "Keep off, Stucki, I've told you . . ."

Stucki caught her arm and held it, laughing. "Next you'll be telling it that you ain't my girl."

"It will be a cold day in hell when I am." She jerked free and Ken took a half step forward.

"That's enough."

Stucki's head snapped around. The rifle was cradled in his left arm and around his waist a belt sagged under the weight of a gun.

"Well now, he'll not only boss the job, he'll make the rules of the house too."

"Let her alone."

The girl surprised him, cutting in. "You keep out of it, mister, I don't need help. Stucki, you go on. You're on shift."

Stucki came around, facing Murdock on his turn toward the door, cocking a finger, aiming it like a gun.

"Just remember, sport, she's mine. I might marry her yet." He went out, laughing, slamming the door carelessly.

The girl put her hands on her hips. "Now, mister, who are you?"

He gave her his name. "Mr. Sheldon hired me as a guard."

The tart tone disapproved. "I'd never have guessed it. An honest miner doesn't need a gun hanging on him. If he has to fight he's got good fists. Go get your duffel, then I'll show you your room."

With that for dismissal, she pivoted and marched off like a bantam cock victorious in the pit. Ken Murdock left the boarding house grinning at his mental picture.

Chapter Five

Ken Murdock walked the town, restless, acquainting himself, bewildered by the electric atmosphere of the boarding house. He had the sense of being shut out, unwanted, and a very long way from home. Even the monotonous layout of the cross streets had a remote austerity that was only partly relieved by their names, women's names chosen alphabetically. He crossed Adele, Bertha, Clara, Dora, Eliza.

Florence was double the width of the others and he turned down it, toward the commercial section. The town of Sutro was booming, the business brisk. Three shifts were working on the tunnel and even as short as funds were the company had so far managed to meet most of its payroll. Only the highest officers were not being paid. But Murdock did not feel a part of it.

He had brought his bedroll back to the boarding house, but the girl had not met him. Jack Bryan, the manager, had taken him up to a room with six bunks. Bryan was obviously Irish, an aging man with a deep limp. Murdock learned later that he was one of the first men hurt in the tunnel and had been given this place as a kind of pension. Most of the boarding houses were company-owned and leased, run as private enterprises.

Bryan was no more cordial than the girl. "There will be no fighting in the house," he had announced. "If you have a quarrel, take it out to the street so the furniture isn't broke. Beer you can bring in but it must be drunk in the front room. Whiskey you do not bring home. Drink it in the saloon and make sure you're not going to be sick before you come here. Supper's at six. You'll hear the gong."

When Bryan had gone, Ken shut the door, changed into his other shirt and pants and took the soiled clothes downstairs. He located the girl in the square kitchen, cutting biscuits on a wooden table beside a huge range, a streak of white flour across her forehead.

"I wonder," he gestured with the clothes, "if I could find someone to wash these." He did not want to explain that what he wore and what he held were all he had.

The deep blue eyes had a snap in them. "You take me for a laundry woman too?"

"Oh no." He hurried. "Isn't there someone around?"

"A Chinaman two blocks down, but he'll do you a poor job. Leave them."

For a moment he didn't understand, then he said, "But I don't want you to do them."

"And indeed why not?"

He opened his mouth, closed it. The last thing he wanted was to get into an argument with this porcupine. He put the clothes down.

"Are you Bryan's daughter?"

"Now you wouldn't take me for his wife? He's over forty."

Lonely, more and more frustrated, he said impulsively, "Why do you dislike me so?"

She met his puzzled gaze fully and it was his eyes that dropped first.

"I neither dislike nor like any of you. I'll have no truck with a man who wears a gun. Fighting, killing, I saw enough of that in San Francisco."

He had been trying to identify her accent. It was not like the Irish along the Klamath, but he had heard that the San Francisco clan had already developed an idiom of its own.

"Ma'am, I've never killed a man in my life."

32

"You will." She ground the cut-out tin can angrily into the flat dough. "A gun makes a murderer sooner or later."

He wanted to protest that his gun was for protection, that but for it Sheldon would now be on a train headed across the snowy Sierras or be dead. He did not. He gave up, turned on his heel and left the building.

It was dark, cold, the spit of snow in the air when he returned. The living room was full of men, the windows steamed, the smell of damp wool and tobacco heavy. He crossed it, climbed the stairs, conscious that the talk and laughter had cut off, guessing that they had heard about his arrival among them and were measuring him, wondering.

He found only one man in the bunkroom, a yellow-haired boy about his own age lying on the bunk next to his, grinning as Ken passed him.

"Hello there."

Ken stopped, wary, neutral. The man sat up and stretched like a lazy cat.

"You must be Murdock."

Ken nodded, saying nothing.

"I'm Al Temple. Bluett said I was to show you the ropes. I hope you like to fight."

The man stood up in a lithe spring. Ken stepped back in reaction, set himself. Temple chuckled.

"Not me, friend. Boris Stucki is laying for you downstairs, cawing that he'll lick you or run you out before the night's over."

Murdock relaxed as inconspicuously as he could. His clothes lay clean and folded on his bunk. He used the minute it took to carry them to the locker and stow them to cover, to think.

"What's Stucki mad at me about?"

"You took his job."

"I didn't know that. From what Bluett said I thought no one was in charge of the guards."

Temple was studying him. Murdock sensed now that the man was neutral, but there was a disconcerting speculation in the green-gray eyes, as if Temple expected him to run now. There was an undertone of wry laughter in his voice.

"Officially no one was in charge. Stucki just declared himself Chief."

"Chief of the company police?"

"Just Chief. You must be new to the Comstock."

"I am."

"Chief's a local term. Back in the early days a blowhard named Brown killed several men, scared the courts, swaggered all over the mountain calling himself Chief, until he got himself killed by a hotelkeeper. The idea caught on and anybody who could bully his way into any leadership took on the title. Stucki is a chief because the rest of the guards, yes and most of the workmen and managers are afraid of him."

Murdock sat down gingerly on the bunk. "Is Sheldon?"

"He is. But he must think you're tough enough to handle Boris or he wouldn't have put you in this spot."

"And you, do you knuckle under?"

"Most assuredly. I was five years old when my father brought me to the mountain. I was raised here, and I'm alive because I keep my head down. I've outlived a lot of chiefs. And this crazy Russian will cripple a man for the pure fun of it. I keep as far as possible out of his way."

"You don't think I can do that?"

"I know you can't. You've got to lick him, kill him or run. There can't be two chiefs on the tunnel."

"Does Bluett know this?"

"Sure, everybody knows it. It was the big talk this afternoon, even the lamp boys and mule skinners were betting on how long it would be before you took off over the hill."

The muscles along Ken Murdock's jaw tightened. "Are you betting I'll run?"

"Why not? You will if you've got any sense. I've seen Stucki ruin four men in the past eight months. Bent the back of one into a pretzel. That's why I waited here. Bryan told me to warn you, he doesn't like trouble in the house."

A bell somewhere on the lower floor caught his attention. "Supper," he said, and his eyes seemed to grow brighter. "You eating or leaving?"

Ken Murdock stood up. "I'm hungry. I never was good at running on an empty stomach."

A long table ran down the center of the dining room, uncovered, the pine top scrubbed to a sheen under the granite plates. Jack Bryan was already seated at one end,

34

Boris Stucki at the other. The Russian's eyes followed Murdock as he came in ahead of Temple. There were two empty chairs close to Bryan's end. Murdock took one, Temple slid into the other.

The board was set with great platters of meat, dishes of potatoes already depleted. The men ranged down the sides were busy eating but watching Murdock furtively. There was tension, as if they waited for a delayed explosion.

Murdock concentrated on the plate before him, turning it upright. A girl, not Sheila, came from the kitchen with a coffeepot, and filled his cup. Murdock waited until she had gone, then followed Temple's lead, reaching with his two-tined iron fork to spear a thick slab of beef from the nearest platter, adding potatoes and biscuits. He ate with his eyes down, silently, steadily, as a man does when his next meal may be a long time away, but he pushed the plate back before it was cleaned. At this moment he did not want to overstuff himself.

Two girls came with trays of pies, dealing a wedge to each man. There had been almost no talk, and that low, brief. He wondered if this was normal or because of his presence.

There was abrupt movement at the far end. He did not look, but sensed that Stucki had shoved to his feet and gone out. He was followed by others as they finished, but Murdock sat where he was until only he and Temple and Bryan were left at the table.

Bryan cleared his throat, his round, red face empty of expression.

"Remember, no fighting in the house."

He rose, pushed open the kitchen door and went through. Murdock looked after him. Temple chuckled lightly.

"It's not too late, friend Murdock. You can get out that way too, get a horse at the livery or walk to Dayton."

"Thanks." Murdock got to his feet deliberately, deliberately unfastened his gun belt. "Hold this for me." He passed the belt and heavy revolver across, turned away from the startled Temple and walked to the living-room door.

Stucki was there, beside the glowing stove, the center of a tight group of men. He had apparently said something funny and they were laughing, his bull roar louder than the rest.

Ken walked toward the group. They saw him and the

35

laughter died. The group parted, backed. Stucki stood alone. His big feet were planted wide apart, his legs looked as thick as redwood trees and as solid, powerful shoulders and bulging arm muscles strained against his shirt.

He watched Murdock with eyes half closed. It made them seem smaller than they were. His head was round, his hair cut short, his heavy cheeks clean-shaven.

Murdock stopped short of Stucki's reach and looked the man over in detail. He did not speak and the Russian grew restive under the silence.

"What do you want?"

Murdock said in an even voice, "They tell me you're a chief."

"I'm *the* Chief."

"I don't think so." Murdock watched him closely. "I hear you've been bragging that you'll run me out or kill me."

Stucki's eyes squirmed even smaller as the red flesh tightened around them. They dropped to Murdock's waist and he showed his first surprise.

"Where's your gun?"

"I don't need a gun to handle you."

Murdock hoped as he said it that it was true. He was afraid. Any man with sense would be afraid, but he knew that he had little choice. He could have run, but aside from crushed pride it would have cost him all chance of recovering his money. His ranch would be irretrievably gone. He could have kept his gun, matched his speed against the bigger man, but he did not want to be shot and he did not want to kill. Sheila's words had tipped his decision; that a man who wore a gun must inevitably kill.

He was risking a brutal beating, but he thought he stood a chance with the Russian. The man was too heavy, his stomach too big, too full. His wind should be poor.

Stucki's surprise faded. He grinned, the ugly mouth stretched wide.

"You're my boy, Murdock. You're my boy." He sounded as if he dearly loved this man. Without looking down, he loosened his gun belt and flung it behind the stove.

From the dining-room door Bryan's voice cut a warning. "Outside. Both of you." He carried a shotgun in his gnarled hands.

Stucki laughed aloud, said to no one in particular, "Sure, Pops. Come on, boys, if you want the show." He swung a big arm and went through the outer door.

Temple spoke behind Murdock in a low tone. "I won't let him stomp you when you go down. That's the way he hurts them, with his feet."

Murdock looked around. Temple had Ken's gun in his hand. His eyes had lost the mockery and were wide, serious. This took more courage than Murdock had thought Temple had. The boy was setting himself to go against the Chief if need be to save Murdock's life.

"Appreciate it," Murdock said, and went out to Boris Stucki.

The Russian had taken a stand in the wide dust track of Tunnel Avenue. The ground was free of snow but frozen into ruts. It made the footing treacherous. Murdock walked out on it. In his shirtsleeves the cold and wind bit at him.

The tunnel guards were crowding out through the door and workmen from the other boarding houses, as if summoned by some mental telegraph, erupted into the street, clustered into a rough circle, leaving an empty field in which Stucki and Murdock faced each other.

Without the gun belt to distort his shape, Murdock saw now, Stucki's arms were overlong for his height. He swung one impatiently.

"Come on, come on, you going to stand there until we freeze?"

Murdock went carefully, feeling the rough footing with his boot soles. His hands ready at his sides, not raised, he moved in.

Without warning, Stucki charged. He came like a bull attacking a fence, both fists swinging, aiming at Murdock's head. At the last instant Murdock jumped aside. The charge carried the Russian past him and Murdock buried a fist deep in the stomach as it hurtled by.

The big man grunted, tried to check the rush, to swing. His doubled hands swept the air as he turned. One jarred against his victim's skull behind the left ear. Murdock hit the square jaw with a force that shot pain lacing through his wrist, into his forearm.

The blow rocked Stucki but did not stop him. He came

37

again, shaking his head to clear his wits, both arms stretched to encircle Murdock.

Ken jumped back. His boot heel caught on the frozen ridge of a deep rut. His ankle turned. He almost fell.

Stucki saw the stumble. With a wordless cry of victory he rushed, careless of any guard, looping heavy blows toward Murdock's head. His right missed, his left cracked into Ken's cheekbone, splitting the skin. Then, as it seemed he must go down, Stucki threw another right. It grazed past Ken's shoulder and the momentum spun the heavier man half around.

Murdock found his balance. He drove a right into the bull neck, came up with a hooking left that caught the chin. Then he put his whole weight behind a right that crushed into Stucki's broad nose, broke the bone, flattened it across the cheeks.

Stucki was blinded for the moment. He groped, pawed wildly for the man he could not see. Murdock backed away, sucking air into his aching lungs. The cheek below his left eye was swelling, his wrist throbbed. He felt that an iron band had been locked around his chest. He ducked a clumsy blow, bent in under it, buried one fist again in the stomach, the other in the neck.

He was in too close. The clawing hands found his shoulders and he was yanked against the thick chest. Stucki was hurt, Stucki was blinded, but he was still dangerous. The arms swept down, grappled around Murdock. The Russian twisted, trying to swing a heel behind Ken's leg and throw him to the ground.

Murdock did not try to break the grip. His left arm was caught but he dragged his right free, pounded at the round head, beat against the neck cord under the big ear.

The vise around his rib cage tightened. He expected the bones to collapse. He tried to bring his knee up into the straddling groin but was too close.

He threw himself sideways, using his weight to hurl them both to the ground. Stucki lit on an elbow. It broke his hold. Murdock rolled clear, fought to his hands and knees, somewhere dredged up the strength to come to his feet.

Stucki too was rising. He was still bent forward when Murdock hit him, a blow that snapped up the bullet head. It did not put the Russian down but it dazed him. He stood like a wounded bear, twisting his head from side to side, searching for his enemy.

Murdock hit him again and then again, sledging one fist to the head, another to the body. It seemed that the blows were utterly futile, that Stucki would never fall.

The throw that rocked the big man back was one of the lightest of the fight, but it caught the chin square, clean, jamming the bloody head back. Stucki sat down. He did not fall, he sank. He sat spread-legged on the frozen ground for a long moment, then he rolled onto his side like a child giving up to sleep.

Murdock stood above him, his legs apart, feet toed in to stay upright, gasping, trying to draw enough air to stop the torture of his lungs, watching for a trick, too dulled to realize that the fight was done, that he had won.

There was sudden silence in the night, a startling change although he had not been conscious of the yelling around him. Temple came forward and took his arm. The crowd stood awed, unbelieving. Then a man moved in slowly, stirred Stucki with his toe, said in a wondering tone, "He's out."

Murdock heard but the words did not register. His mind was closed in a numb haze that veiled him away from the world.

Temple kept repeating, "You licked him. You licked him. You're the new Chief."

It meant nothing to Murdock. The crowd separated to let them through. Murdock did not notice. The roaring in his head would not stop. The cut in his cheek leaked blood that tickled down his skin. The flesh around the cut was swelling and the eye above it would not open properly.

He felt the rush of heat as Temple opened the door, pushed and steered him into the living room. It was like a fever after the outdoor cold.

He heard a voice say, "Bring him in here."

He located the red moon of Bryan's face and let Temple guide him through the dining room, into the kitchen.

"Put him there." Bryan pointed to a chair beside the kitchen table.

Temple eased him into the seat. The ache in his lungs had begun to subside, the haze over his vision was clearing gradually, and now the hurts his body had sustained set up their cry as consciousness returned. He had been out on his feet, stupified by complete exhaustion. If the fight had lasted minutes longer he would have fallen in sheer fatigue.

Someone was standing over him, came into focus as Sheila, holding a pan of steaming water. She put the pan on the table, dipped a cloth into it and ran it gently over his beaten face. Pain almost made him scream. The soft linen fibers felt like the ragged teeth of a file. He gasped aloud when she used a piece of alum to stanch the bleeding cut.

"Sit still. Quit acting like a baby."

He tried to glare at her with his good eye. It was not successful. She continued mopping him off. When his face was cleaned to her satisfaction she stood back.

"Now take off that shirt."

He had never yet taken off a shirt in the presence of a woman. He made no move.

"Come on, you lout, off with it."

Unwillingly he stood up, his ears reddening as he discovered Al Temple and Bryan across the table, the two waitresses beside the sink, all grinning at him.

He fumbled with the buttons, the knuckles of his right hand badly swollen. Impatiently Sheila shoved his fingers aside, unfastened the shirt and peeled it from him. She held it up in disgust, bloody, torn, grime ground into it.

"Look at this thing. I suppose you're proud of it, so pleased with yourself. You licked Boris Stucki. That makes you a big man. Big man."

"And not with a gun." Murdock managed to wedge it in.

She tossed her head, flung the shirt toward a waitress. "Betsey, put the rag to soak in cold water. Don't use hot, it will set the stains. Al, go upstairs and bring him a fresh shirt. I know he's got one, I washed it this afternoon. Then take him over to Doc Hazlett."

Murdock's male pride was as badly mauled as his body. He said stubbornly, "I don't need a doctor."

Her eyes flashed with scorn. "Don't be a bigger fool than the good Lord made you. Do you want an infection from that street filth?"

J.C. Hazlett, like so many of Sutro's employees, served in several capacities. He was at once physician for the tunnel company, assayer for any rock that might show ore values

40

along the bore, and head of the stock-selling office Sutro maintained in Dayton. Overworked, short-tempered, sarcastic, his greeting to Temple and Murdock was brusque and without sympathy. Word of the fight had already reached him, spreading in a shock wave through the community.

"So you're the bucko who whipped Boris Stucki."

"Has the Russian bum been here? How is he?" Temple's words still held laughter.

"He'll recover." Hazlett sounded as if he regretted it. "You can't kill an animal by hitting it in the head with your fists. But he won't be working for a few days. Let me look at that hand."

Ken Murdock held it out. It was swelled twice its normal size.

The doctor snorted. "Not much you can do for it except soak it in hot water three or four times a day." He dropped the hand and prodded at the cheek, then swabbed it ungently with iodine.

Murdock bit off his yell and stinging tears clouded his eyes. Hazlett was not moved.

"You'll have a scar from that, but who hasn't. Keep it clean. That'll be ten dollars."

Ken Murdock stiffened. "Ten dollars?"

"It's a night call. Five in the daytime."

Al Temple protested. "You're supposed to be the company doctor."

"That's right. Sutro pays me to take care of any accident on the job. He doesn't pay for somebody getting banged up in a fight on his own time."

Al Temple was not so easily put off. Ken was to learn that the yellow-haired man was a born bunkhouse lawyer with a love of argument.

"Murdock had to fight Stucki. Sheldon hired him and put him in charge. He couldn't have stayed on that job unless he beat the Russian clown."

Hazlett shrugged. "Not an official on-the-job affair. The fee is ten dollars."

"Which I won't have until payday." Murdock was embarrassed, wished the girl had not butted in, that Temple was not witness to his plight.

But Temple had only begun. "Look, Doc, the office takes

41

two dollars every week out of our pay. Sutro calls it health insurance. You know about it, you know the miners' union raised hell about it last year but it's still taken. Who gets that money? You or Sutro?"

"I don't get it directly. I bill the company for any accident I take care of."

"Then I'm going to talk to Sutro about it."

"You do that. And when you see him give him my regards. I've been trying to catch him for a month to ask him some questions of my own."

Temple made a sour face. Sutro was seldom in the vicinity these days. When he wasn't in Europe trying to pry more money out of the McCalmont banking group he was in Washington defending the tunnel before Congressional committees or in San Francisco dickering for the precious agreements with the directors of the mining companies.

"Where is he now?"

Hazlett flapped his hands. "San Francisco I guess. He's supposed to be back next week. Who the hell knows?" He sat down at his desk, scribbled on a small blank, pushed it toward Murdock. "Sign this, please."

"What is it?" Since the foreclosure of his ranch mortgage Ken Murdock had been very leery of signing any paper.

"An order on the company authorizing Sheldon to deduct ten dollars from your pay."

Ken Murdock signed, but his swollen hand made the name almost unreadable.

Chapter Six

Ken Murdock's first two weeks on the job were a brutal trial, but he stayed with it. The pace of the work at the face had speeded up and in his time there the three shifts punched more than a hundred feet further into the heart of the mountain.

The heat intensified. Murdock barely tolerated it for days,

then grew accustomed to it, to the noxious gasses, the deafening hammer of the drills, the sight of a dead mule now hauled out on nearly every shift.

He had become acquainted with the men of the tunnel police force. There were twenty of them including himself and seven were on duty through each eight-hour stretch, one at the entrance, one at the office, one in the change room and four strung a mile apart along the tunnel. Their responsibility covered any emergency that arose; if an air hose to the drills failed, get it fixed immediately; if a blower fouled, get it cleared at once; if a mule dropped dead in harness, haul it out and bring up another to move the car; if a dispute broke out, settle it fast. Nothing was to hold up the work.

There were many fights. Men laboring in temperatures of a hundred and ten to twenty, half smothered by the fumes of powder shots and gasses accumulated over the ten years, were short of temper. Even normally they were rough men, given to violence, heavy drinking, quick grievances. No other kind could survive this sweltering hell.

Both Sheldon and Bluett had made it plain that Murdock's first duty was to protect the bulkhead, but he found that he had others as well, as head of the guards. He had had no trouble with them. His fight with the Russian had given him the right to control, and even Stucki appeared to bow to his leadership.

Boris had turned up for work on the third day, his face still battered, but surprisingly showing no rancor. He came into the office where Murdock was drawing up the schedule. Murdock looked up warily from the desk, watched the bulky man cross the rough board floor toward him. Stucki was grinning but Murdock was not reassured. The Russian stopped, looming above the desk.

"Well, sport, it takes a somebody to knock me over."

Murdock said nothing, waited to see how this was going to turn. He was still feeling his way, trying to learn exactly what his job involved. He had just made Al Temple foreman of the four-to-midnight shift and was debating who should head up the other two.

Stucki rubbed at the swelling on his left jaw. "Yes, by God, you licked me good."

The others in the office had turned to watch, wondering if

the fight would start again here. The Russian walked around Murdock's desk, flung his huge arm across Ken's shoulder.

"I never got licked before and maybe if we did it over I wouldn't then. But I had enough, let's forget it, sport, as far as I'm concerned you're the Chief."

Murdock let his breath out slowly, hiding it, sitting back away from the man.

"How would you like to be foreman of the twelve to eight?"

The big man lowered his head, pushing his face forward. "You mean that?"

"Ten dollars a month extra." Murdock hoped that Sheldon would back him up. He wasn't sure, but he needed loyal support from his foremen.

"That's real handsome," Stucki said. "You're a gent and no mistake. I'm your man, boss." His grin widened, looking around at the eavesdropping clerks. "Any of you pen pushers give my friend trouble, I'll tie you in a knot."

He walked out, his old swagger recovered. Murdock turned back to his work, relaxing, feeling that he was beginning to understand how to handle a crew. And in the next two weeks his hunch had proven right. There had not been a single fight on Stucki's twelve to eight.

It had taken some argument, but Sheldon had agreed to the bonus for the foremen and approved Ken's decision to station the foreman of each shift at the bulkhead, and he called on Ken for further services. In the third week he came to the office saying, "I want you to drive up the mountain with me, bring another guard, one you trust most. We have to pick up the payroll."

Murdock got his coat, went to the boarding house for Al Temple, then on to the livery where Sheldon was already waiting in a company buckboard. It was a cold ride up the canyon to the Wells Fargo office at Gold Hill, where the money was loaded into the mud wagon. Snow swirled around them on the return trip, but it was with a warm feeling that Murdock helped stow the funds in the big company safe, and watched Sheldon spin the dials.

"Payday," said the tunnel executive, "will start tomorrow morning. As of this moment we have thirteen hundred and ten employees. It will take about five days. Adjust your schedule so that you can stand guard."

It puzzled Murdock why the pay-out should take so long. He found out next day. Every workman had to show his pay slip before he was admitted to Sheldon's office. Sheldon sat at his desk behind a tray stacked with twenty-dollar gold pieces, other trays of smaller coins. The miners came in a single file, thirty permitted in at a time, passing a clerk who checked the slips and gave Sheldon each amount.

From each man's total Sheldon first made deductions. To David Biggs, collector for the poll tax imposed by Dayton, to Garnett the subscriptions for the hospital fund, to Hubert of the Miners' Union, who made certain each man had a union card. The miner was given the rest. But not to take away with him. There were other demands on the money.

Seated around the edge of the room were the boarding house keepers, restaurant men, saloon people. Each had his credit book and a revolver. The miner must pass these creditors before he could reach the door, and few among them had not run up a bill in some of these establishments.

Arguments added to the delay. Many miners had given false names in obtaining credit. The merchants had to depend on a memory for faces as well as their books. Murdock's job of keeping order was not easy. There were scuffles more or less violent. One man tried to rush past the gauntlet and was shot by a saloonkeeper over a debt of twelve dollars.

Ken Murdock, one of the last to step to the desk, found that Doctor Hazlett had indeed put in his claim for ten dollars, and Jack Bryan waited like a hawk with his board bill of fourteen.

When that was paid they walked together as far as the boarding house. Bryan turned in but Murdock went on to town. He needed clothes, and most of his remaining pay went for socks, flannel underwear, shirts, and a suit of black worsted from the Bon Ton Store that Smiling Sam Levine assured him was the latest fashion on Montgomery Street in distant San Francisco.

Jack Bryan carried the small carpetbag in which he collected his rents to the safe in the living room, locked it up, then went on to the kitchen where Sheila was supervising the preparation of the evening meal. Her cheeks were red from the heat of the big range, her eyes concerned.

"Did you collect them all?"

Bryan nodded, unbuckling his gun belt, hanging it on the wall peg.

"From Stucki even?"

Jack Bryan grinned. "He paid up like a lamb, never a whimper. That Murdock's made a Christian out of him."

"And Murdock?"

"Forked over without a question. He's a nice boy. A lot of men would have thrown their weight around if they'd licked Boris. Murdock acts like people are doing him a favor just to let him live here."

She sniffed. "He wears a gun."

Her father said mildly, "I wear a gun when I go to collect."

"That's different. These men, any man—give him coins in his pocket and he'll head for the nearest saloon and devil take the folks he owes. You work for your money. People like Murdock strut around with their guns while their betters swing a pick."

"You've really got it in for him, haven't you?"

She turned from him, opened the oven door and lifted in a huge roast. "He means nothing at all to me. I've no respect for someone who won't bend his back and do an honest day's work."

"He's worked plenty." Bryan helped himself to a fresh sugar cookie from the fat jar on the cupboard shelf. "He built up a good ranch in Oregon, by himself. He only came here because his brother sold their cattle and then put the money in tunnel stock and the bank called his loan, took his ranch."

"Who told you that? It's a fine sad story and I'll bet there's not a word of truth in it."

"You've got no call to say that. Al Temple told me, says Murdock's trying to earn enough to buy back the ranch. Al says Murdock has offered him a job when he does and Al thinks he'll take it."

Sheila made herself busy with supper as if to cut off any more talk on the subject. Her father finished his cookie, poured himself a cup of coffee and watched her with a thoughtful frown.

Sheila worried him. Her mother had died five years ago and the child had taken over here, only thirteen. He had not liked the arrangement, did not now. Forty men lived in the house, most of them unmarried, most in their twenties or early thirties. Work in the tunnel was not for the middle-aged.

Many of them had been away from home five to ten years. Their only feminine contact was with the women of the cribs below D Street in Virginia. It was not a wholesome place for a growing girl, especially a pretty one, and he couldn't watch her every minute.

From the first she had proved that she could look out for herself and she had shown no marked interest in any of the boarders, but she was nearing an age when some man would capture her awakening attention.

Jack Bryan had been a full-blooded man. He knew what biology could do to the most level-headed female. And positive a girl as she was, when someone did appear and turn her head, that would be the end of it.

Not that he did not want her to marry, but he dreaded that it could be one of his boarders. As a lot they were drifters who would never make more than the four dollars a day that was standard for underground work on the lode.

To forestall such a thing he had tried for the last year to persuade her to go to his sister in San Francisco, where she would stand a chance of meeting someone other than miners. She had flatly refused to leave him, arguing that without her he could not run the boarding house.

Painfully, she was right. These guards with their guns could cause deep trouble. She joshed them along, kept them at arm's length, babied them when they were sick, fed them better than any other group in Sutro. On Saturday nights she played the organ in the living room, served cookies and coffee, danced with them when someone would play the fiddle. The result was that the Saturday night drinking bouts had been cut sharply.

It was hell, Jack Bryan told himself, for a father to try to judge a prospect for a marriageable daughter. The qualities

47

one man recognized in another were not necessarily what would attract a woman.

He was particularly uneasy about Al Temple. The yellow-haired boy had a devil-may-care breeziness, a charm that had the waitresses giggling and blushing. Now there was the uncertainty about Murdock. Sheila's attitude toward him was too intense.

There was none of Temple's recklessness in Murdock. He was a quiet, steady worker as far as Bryan could tell. But his prospects were less than impressive. If the Oregon ranch could be regained they might look better, although Bryan had seen enough of the small hard-scrabble outfits to have little faith in their potential. But without the ranch Murdock couldn't hope to be more than a forty-dollar-a-month cowhand. Even a miner earned more than twice that, at least when he worked.

Unhappy with his thoughts he wandered to the living room, shoved fresh wood in the stove. With the damn wind and the dropping temperature it would be a miserable night, probably would snow.

The opening door brought a chill blast and Murdock, his arms filled with packages. The men did not trouble to speak, they had seen each other only an hour before.

Ken climbed the stairs and went back along the hall. It was early and the room was empty. He laid out the new suit on the bed, admiring it there for a moment, then he shucked off his work clothes and tried it on.

It was the first real suit he had owned and he posed before the fogged mirror over the washstand, deciding that maybe Smiling Sam had told the truth. To him it looked as good as the clothes worn by the travelers on the train.

He straightened the coat, picked up a package and used the rear stairs down to the kitchen.

The room was warm, friendly with the smells of cookery. Sheila Bryan sat at the scrubbed table, a cup of tea before her, resting until it would be time to put the biscuits in the oven. The waitresses had not yet come and she was alone.

She looked toward the stairs, startled as he came in, tricked into a quick smile that was gone almost at once.

"My, aren't you the dandy on payday."

He was pleased but too embarrassed to show it. He crossed

to the table and laid the package before her. Her brows lifted and she raised her eyes to his, faint color touching her cheeks.

"What's that?"

"For doing my washing."

She leaned back away from the box as if it might explode. "I didn't do your washing for pay."

He fumbled. "It isn't that. It's—a kind of gift."

Still she made no move to touch it. Disappointment rode through him. He had not known exactly what he had expected, almost afraid to make the offering for fear of offending her. He had a hearty respect for her unpredictable temper.

"Please, just open it."

She saw the look on his face, suddenly pulled a knife from the table drawer and cut the colored string, peeled back the paper. Inside was a pound box of Sellers chocolates.

She dropped the knife, folded her hands in her lap and stared at the box, for the moment unable to speak. She well knew what it had cost. A whole dollar. Twice she hunted words that her tight throat muscles would not utter. This was the first gift from a man she had ever received.

"I—I—" For defense she resorted to scolding. "Now isn't that just like a man—throwing your money away. You come in here broke, you've got only two shirts, two pair of pants —" she did not tell him she had checked his locker. "You get a job and the first pay you draw you waste on fancy Dan clothes and candy."

She bit her lip. She wanted to cry. She had not meant to say that, but she could not keep from adding, "Is this the way you expect to get your ranch back?"

He choked, his mind empty of an answer. Then he was saved by someone shouting his name from the front room. He fled.

Behind him the girl sat hypnotized by the box. Then she lowered her head onto her arms crossed over the gift. For the first time since her mother's death she cried.

One of the lamp boys stood at the bottom of the stairs, shouting up them as Ken Murdock ran from the dining room.

"What is it? What's happened?"

"Mr. Sheldon wants you in the office, quick."

Murdock's instinctive thought was of trouble at the tunnel. He raced up the stairs, did not take the time to change clothes, flapped his gun belt around his waist, grabbed his heavy coat and went down the steps three at a time. The boy had already gone. Murdock dived for the door, pounded up the frozen street.

Sheldon was at his office desk, in his usual fussy mood, nothing of emergency in his manner.

"You'll have to drive up to Virginia. Sutro is at the International Hotel—at least he was due on the evening train—and the damn telegraph lines are out again. Every time I have to send a message up there the wires are down."

Murdock was breathless from the run, watching Sheldon fold and seal a sheet of stationery and pass it toward him.

"This note will explain, but I'd better tell you what it is in case you have trouble. Tell Sutro we are now right under the sixteen-hundred-foot level of the Savage. Their afternoon blasts shook the tunnel roof and the crew is scared to death."

"That I know."

"Find out what Sutro wants us to do—stop work until he gets his agreement signed or keep digging. It's a rotten night and going to get worse. You may have to lay over there, but see me as soon as you get back. If I'm not here, come over to my house. You'll have to hurry if you're going to beat the snow."

Murdock tucked the note into his shirt pocket, buttoned his coat over it and left. Coming up the hill the wind had been at his back. It was directly in his face as he hurried to the livery and he was chilled in spite of the sheep-lined coat before he reached the shelter of the barn.

The hostler, putting the horses to the buckboard, said, "Coldest February I can remember. I got some stones heating on the stove."

He brought them wrapped in a blanket, put them in the wagon under Ken's feet and tossed a buffalo robe up. Ken wrapped himself in it and turned the rig down Tunnel Avenue toward the old overland trail that would take him down river to Dayton.

The climb up the canyon to Gold Hill was bitter. Ken's teeth were rattling when he came into the small city and swung the team into the livery runway. Gratefully he drank coffee from the hostler's steaming pot, thawed out while the animals rested. Their breath had frozen around their heads like white nightcaps. When he moved them back into the windy street they dogged. He had to use the whip to get them over the divide and down C Street to the barn across from the hotel.

His face burned, his fingers would not close when he came into the warm lobby. His lips were stiff as he asked the clerk behind the mahogany desk for Adolph Sutro.

The clerk held him there, sending a bellman to ask if Sutro would receive the messenger. Murdock had not been inside the International before. He used the waiting time to look around the big room in disbelief, at the arched ceiling, the ornate overhead chandeliers, the full walls of mirrors that reflected overstuffed chairs, sofas, polished, glowing tables. The hotel was barely two years old and said to be the finest structure between Chicago and San Francisco. Certainly it had the most impressive elevators west of New York City.

One of the hydraulic, mirrored cars lifted Ken to the sixth floor where a square-built man waited in the corridor. There was authority in the bulky figure. The forehead was high, the hairline far back. The upper lip was hidden behind a luxurious mustache, giving the illusion of a receding chin, an impression heightened by bushy sideburns following down his jaws and joining the mustache.

"I don't know you." The voice was guttural with a German accent, but not cold.

It was, Ken had no doubt, Adolph Sutro himself, the remote man he had come to Nevada to find, the man from whom he had hoped to recover his money. But he was unlike the conflicting pictures gossip had built in his mind.

The man fired strong reactions in those who knew him. To the miners on the lode he was a sort of god who fought for their safety and well-being. To the mineowners, profit greedy, hating to think of paying out a royalty on their ore, he was a robber. The merchants of Virginia, Gold Hill, Silver City, their businesses threatened if the mills were moved down to the river, saw him as a devil to be fought with all the influence and power at their command.

Ken Murdock saw a man he instinctively trusted in spite of

his preconceived suspicion. He introduced himself and extended Sheldon's note.

Without opening it, Sutro beckoned with it, led Murdock down the carpeted hall to the corner rooms he used when he was in town.

In the sitting room a dining table was laid with white linen, sparkling glass, glowing silverware. A meal had just been finished. Across the table sat a woman, an expensive woman in a blue dress with a small fur collar.

Sutro did not introduce her but Ken Murdock guessed who she was. Everyone on the mountain whispered about Mrs. George Allen, called her the ninety-thousand-dollar widow although Ken had never heard an explanation. She was a tempting subject for gossip, a mystery. It was not known where she came from or why she chose to stay in the mining camp, although rumor said she had been a friend of Sutro's long before she burst on the Virginia scene.

Certainly Mrs. Sutro believed that rumor. A favorite story among the tunnel workmen told about the night Leah Sutro had invaded the International Hotel and smashed a bottle of champagne against Mrs. Allen's head, and it further endeared the tunnel king to them. Full-bodied men, they delighted that their hero suffered the same weaknesses of the flesh they did.

Mrs. Allen did not look up but sat quietly, her hands folded in her lap, her eyes on her plate. Sutro lowered himself into the chair opposite her and read Sheldon's note, tapped it against his thumb, said with obvious satisfaction, "So. It is nearly finished."

"I guess so." Murdock did not know whether Sutro was addressing him or talking to himself.

"Finished." The man took a long, deep breath as if he were drinking it. Murdock had a flashing glimpse of the grinding strain of the long years.

Sutro frowned suddenly. "Why didn't Sheldon use the telegraph?"

"The wires are dead, maybe they're down. There's a lot of ice."

"Yes, always when we need them most. Is it cold outside?"

"Very cold."

"Then stay in Virginia tonight. It is no use to freeze. Tell Sheldon the crew should enlarge the station but not to break

52

through into the Savage. Do not break through until I give the word. I am meeting with the Savage people again tomorrow. If their miners should break through, have Sheldon block the opening. He must keep it blocked until the agreement is signed. Do you understand?"

Murdock nodded.

"He is to let me know at once if it happens. That is all."

Sutro dismissed him with a wave of the hand. Murdock started for the door, then stopped. Here was his chance and he must risk speaking, even if Sutro resented it and had him fired.

"I'd like to talk to you about something else."

"Of course." Sutro turned to look at him squarely. Seldom in his life had he made friends of his own level but to his employees he was kind, understanding, ready to listen. He was attentive now as Ken detailed his story.

"I want that ranch back, Mr. Sutro." His tone was low, not threatening, but held a stubborn doggedness.

Sutro recognized it and measured Murdock expertly. Behind him lay a lot of experience with disgruntled investors, a full range between the British banking house of the McCalmont brothers who held a nine-hundred-and-ninety-seven-thousand-dollar mortgage on the tunnel property and the four-dollar miner who had bought a single share. He stood up, came to Murdock and laid a hand on Ken's shoulder solidly.

"I know, I know. It is a shocking loss."

Of anyone else Murdock would have been suspicious, but his new image of this man, something in the eyes, direct and candid, gave him the sense that Sutro was honest in his concern.

"Believe me, boy, if it were possible I would return your money tonight." Adolph Sutro sighed. "There is so much I would choose to do. Bear with us a little longer. When we are in operation your stock will be worth more than it cost. A short while more. The owners are tricky and will squirm as they have so long. But we will win.

"Remember to tell Sheldon not to allow a breakthrough, but if the mine does it, to plug the hole. Do not allow a single Savage man into the tunnel. Be ready to close the bulkhead at any moment should they try to flood us. That's your job, and depending on how well you do it is how soon you will recover."

All the time he talked he held Murdock's shoulder, steering him out to the hall, down it to the elevators. Not until he was dropping toward the lower level did Murdock see how adroitly Sutro had gotten rid of him, and anger hit him that he had let himself be so maneuvered. He was a lamb here among sophisticated wolves.

He came out of the car uncertain where to turn. Most of his money had gone for clothes and the gift for Sheila. He could not afford this hotel. He thought of the cheap boarding house he had checked into the first night and had left so precipitously when he and Sheldon had fled the town.

As he stood, a second elevator opened and a voice said, "Why, Mr. Murdock." He looked up and saw Helen Powell coming out. He pulled off his hat as she came toward him, her uncle a step behind her.

"I thought you must have left Virginia. You didn't come to see us."

He was flustered. "I did, sort of. I got a job with the tunnel company. As a guard."

"You've been upstairs? You've talked to Crazy Adolph about your stock?"

"Well, I tried. Mr. Sheldon sent me up with a message and it gave me a chance ..."

Helen Powell turned her head, met her uncle's eyes. For days there had been increasing whispers that Sutro and the Savage company were nearing agreement. If it was really, finally going to be signed—if they had advance notice they could step in, buy the nearly worthless stock and make a fortune. She laid a gloved hand on Murdock's arm.

"I'm so happy to see you. I was afraid you'd gone back to Oregon without even stopping in to say goodbye. You'll dine with us, of course?"

Henry Powell was not as quick-witted as his niece. His surprise showed, but Helen cut off any chance of his flubbing this. "If you haven't been to the French Rotisserie you've never eaten."

Ken Murdock felt trapped. An invitation from this dazzling girl was beyond his hope. But he had three dollars in his pocket and the suit that had seemed so right earlier seemed

54

out of style and shoddy compared to the clothes in this lobby.

"I'm afraid I have to get back to Sutro. I've got word for Mr. Sheldon and . . ."

Helen Powell was not about to let him go. Here was a God-given opportunity to pry out what Sutro and his lieutenants were up to.

"Make him come with us, Henry. We surely owe him a dinner for protecting me on the train."

Henry Powell had got the idea. "We won't hear of your refusing, Mr. Murdock. Helen and I were wondering only today how you had made out."

Each of them holding an arm, they took possession of Ken Murdock.

The restaurant was still another new experience to Ken Murdock, the quiet elegance of the room, the low lights, the soft-footed waiters, the delicate food. He had been spared the ordeal of trying to order from a menu in French. Henry Powell ordered for them all. Now Murdock sat sipping wine and talking more than he had ever talked in his life.

Helen Powell was artful in drawing people out. He described his meeting with Sheldon, his being hired, his run-in with Boris Stucki. He minimized the fights, but out of his own interest he explained the bulkhead, the problems of the work, the difficulties with the mules. The one area he did not touch on was Sheila Bryan. For some dim reason he found it impossible to mention the girl's name to Helen Powell. He had a rapt audience and he was flattered by Helen's knowledgeable questions.

"Where does it stand now between Sutro and the mines? Has the Savage signed?"

It did not occur to Murdock that he was not supposed to talk about such things to anyone not a member of the tunnel management, particularly a stockbroker.

"He hasn't. They're threatening to turn their sump water into the tunnel without paying."

"Oh dear. What would happen then?"

Murdock moved his shoulders. "Jack Bluett says if they did that the hot water could eat out the clay that's behind a lot of the timbering and cave the tunnel. But there's the bulkhead to stop it. We think it will hold against all the water they can throw against it. That's about the whole story up to now."

Henry Powell pulled his watch. The restaurant was nearly empty.

"I think it's about time we broke this up. I have to be at the Change early tomorrow. Our carriage is outside, can we drop you somewhere?"

Ken Murdock refused that offer. He did not want them knowing he was staying at the boarding house.

At the door the girl extended her hand. "Promise you will come to see me the next time you're in Virginia. And do write to me, tell me what you're doing, what's happening in the tunnel."

"If you're interested . . ."

"I am very interested." She leaned toward him, lowered her tone so that it did not reach her uncle. "In you. In everything you're doing."

Chapter Seven

The morning was clear and cold, the team freshened and ready to go. Ken Murdock drove them automatically, unaware of anything around him. His mind kept going over the night before in wonderment.

First, he had met and talked with Adolph Sutro. He had not gotten his nine thousand dollars and he felt that he had been expertly brushed off, but he was still impressed. There was a great magnetism about Sutro that had made itself felt from the United States Congress and the big European bankers to the lowliest mucker on his payroll.

And on top of that interview had come the heady reception given him by Helen Powell and her uncle. On the train he had felt a strong attraction to her and she had been politely friendly, but he had not dared to believe that she would remember him, let alone take him to dinner and show a lively interest in what he was doing.

If he had been present at a meeting that was even then taking place at the Powell brokerage office his present good opinion of himself would have taken a wound.

Half a dozen men sat around the conference table but Helen, at the head, dominated the room. They were some of the most active brokers on the Comstock. They lived in an air of constant excitement, for the fluctuation of the stocks listed on the mining exchange was always active and violent. The key to this group's success was inside information. Much of their time and money was spent in trying to get to the men underground in the various mines, in bribing shift bosses and foremen to tip them off when a new strike was made that would sharply increase a mine's earning power. They worked independently, secretively, jealously, but they had all jumped to gather here at Helen Powell's hint that she knew something of interest.

"As you know we've never been able to get to anyone close to Sutro," she told them. "Crazy Adolph and his clique are the tightest-mouthed people on the Lode. But now I have a young man, the head of Sutro's tunnel police." She paused, her eyes bright, giving time for the men to consider the implication of her words, and then went on, "Apparently Sheldon trusts him. He uses him as a messenger to Sutro. Jack Bluett trusts him. And he spent an hour with Adolph last night."

They were listening, weighing. They had learned that behind the femininity of her appearance this girl had as shrewd a business sense as any man among them.

"The word is that the mineowners are not going to sign the tunnel contracts. The whisper is that they mean to pump their sumps into the tunnel as soon as a connection is made. If they do that Sutro is ruined, the tunnel company is through. But . . ."

She smiled, letting the word hang in the air. "But supposing Sutro is ready for that. Suppose he has built a bulkhead to block the water and force it back up into the mines . . .?"

A man named Foss let his breath out slowly. "Does such a bulkhead exist?"

"I am told it does."

"Your young friend?"

She nodded.

"How do you know you can trust him? It could be a fake leak of Sutro's to make a market for his stock."

She laughed, looking at her uncle. "What do you think, Henry?"

Henry Powell's lip curled. "The boy is a bumpkin. He had a ranch in Oregon and he lost it because his brother put their cattle money into tunnel stock. He's infatuated by Helen. He'll answer anything she wants to ask. You can be assured he is not part of any stock manipulation scheme."

Foss's voice was dry. "I judge this information is not gratis. What do you want?"

"To form a syndicate, and when I give the word, start buying tunnel stock. I could do it myself, but a single broker operating would rouse suspicion. With all of us buying gradually we should be able to pick up what is lying around for a song. That bulkhead will force the mines to sign, and when they do the stock will go through the sky. Are you with us?"

There was no hesitation. Henry Powell called a clerk, dictated an agreement and watched the men sign it.

Ken Murdock was not aware of the new syndicate. He was whistling when he drove into the livery barn at eleven o'clock, left the team and walked to Sheldon's office. He delivered Sutro's message and hummed as he went on to the boarding house to change his clothes.

He found Sheila Bryan cleaning the front room, a cloth tied around her hair to keep the dust from it, one escaped lock glistening in the sun that came through the windows.

She faced him, folding her hands on her hips, surveying him. There was a surprising welcome in her eyes but her bluster belied it.

"So you had to rush up to Virginia to throw away the rest of your money."

Feeling as good as he did he grinned and scaled his hat up the stair well. "I had to go up to see Mr. Sutro."

"A fine story." She sniffed. "And what would Adolph Sutro be wanting with the likes of you?"

"Not with me, exactly. I took a message up for Mr. Sheldon and it was so cold Sutro said I was to stay the night."

"And I suppose he gave you a part of his bed."

"He didn't." Murdock laughed aloud. "He had a lady there

58

and—" he cut off quickly. He had not meant to say that. Color came up under his heavy tan and he started to stutter.

Sheila clapped one hand across her mouth, choking back an explosion, coughed and almost strangled as she fought against laughter.

"You—" she said when she could speak. "Would you mean you saw Mrs. Allen there?"

Murdock's face burned. "I shouldn't have said—I don't know who she was—only that she was pretty—and what does a child like you know about Mrs. Allen?"

Sheila gasped for breath and composure, shaking her head over him. "What a ninny. And why wouldn't I know about Mrs. Allen? The whole camp talks. What do you think women talk about, Mr. Ken Murdock?"

"I—I don't know. I don't know much about women."

"You don't know much about anything, Mr. Man. You are the green one, you are. Women talk about other women, that's what, and men are simple not to know it. You all treat a woman as if she didn't have eyes in her head or ears to hear or the sense to know what's going on. You're as bad as my father."

"But you shouldn't talk about . . ."

"And why shouldn't I? The men talk. And roll their eyes and smirk and say things sly so they think I don't understand what they mean. Well, little boy, I'll venture I know a lot more about the facts of life than you do, so don't pull that high and mighty male act on me. Did Sutro ask you to supper?"

"No. I went with Helen Powell and her uncle."

Her last words had been easier, conversational, unashamedly curious, and she had begun sweeping the floor as if settling in for a pleasant gossip. When he answered, she stopped, straightened and looked him up and down.

"Now isn't the man just full of surprises. And why did Helen Powell go to dinner with you?"

"She didn't. I mean, she and her uncle took me—to a French restaurant."

The heavy lashes around her eyes closed nearly together and she peered at him intently. "When did you meet those people?"

Her tone astonished him, made him feel like a small boy

59

being interrogated by his mother, and he answered her with the boy's sense of some mysterious guilt.

"I met her on the train and she asked me to come to see her. She's a stockbroker and ..."

"And I know very well who she is. Everybody knows. An unwed woman working in a business office just like a man."

Annoyance came up in him and he said sharply, "Why shouldn't she? There's nothing wrong with her working there if she's smart enough to handle it."

"Oh, isn't there? I suppose you haven't heard any of the things they say about her?"

"I have not and I don't want to."

"Well let me tell you, Mr. Murdock, that people talk about her just the way they talk about Mrs. Allen. She ..."

She stopped. Murdock had turned to the stairs and was running up them. Sheila Bryan slammed the broom bristles against the floor.

"Well I never." She was talking to herself. "Go on, get yourself mixed up with that floozy and see if I care." She spun and fled into the dining room.

Ken Murdock spent the next several days avoiding Sheila as much as possible, but mealtimes were a problem. Twice more Sheldon sent him to Virginia with messages for Sutro, and he stole time to visit the Powell office. The warm reception he had there was heightened by Sheila's pointed coolness on his return.

Jack Bryan watched the growing strain between them and did not mention it. Al Temple watched, and finally caught Murdock at the bulkhead alone. In a troubled voice he said, "What's going on between you and Sheila?"

Murdock turned slowly to face him, and made no answer.

Temple was half angry, half embarrassed. "Maybe you think it isn't my business, but I'm telling you it is."

Murdock raised his eyebrows. "Why?"

They eyed each other like hostile strangers, ready to fight. Then Temple drew a ragged breath.

"I've been trying to get that girl to marry me for a long time, way back before you showed up."

Murdock turned back to the hinge he was oiling. "Go to it. Marry her and good luck."

Behind him there was deep unhappiness in Temple's voice. "I said I was trying. She says she won't have me."

Murdock did not look around and his own embarrassment roughened his tone. "What am I supposed to have to do with it?"

"I'm asking you to let her alone."

Murdock turned then, almost ready to smile. "I'm trying to do exactly that, but she's got a sharp tongue and she wants to boss everybody. What have I done wrong?"

"You gave her a box of candy."

Ken Murdock laughed. "For God sake, Al, she did me a favor and I wanted to return it. There was nothing more to it."

The blond man did not relax, but thrust out his chin belligerently while his face reddened.

"Then why did I catch her crying over it? Murdock, you've got one girl on the string, don't reach for this one."

Murdock was perfectly still. His impulse was to grab Temple by his shirt front and shake him. He held his breath for a full minute before he could speak fairly calmly.

"What do you mean by that?"

"Helen Powell. You're seeing her. Fred Grove saw her with you at the Rotisserie the other night, and yesterday when I rode up town with you, you couldn't wait to get to her office."

Murdock barely kept his fist from swinging. "That," he said, "I consider to be my business."

"That part, yes, you do any damn thing you want. But Sheila you leave alone. Understand?"

Temple swung away and walked stiffly down the tunnel. Murdock started to call after him, then shrugged. Temple was as close to a friend as he had made on the Comstock, but there were personal matters that one man simply did not discuss with another.

He began to calm down, thinking of Helen Powell. She was like no one else he had ever met. Some women seem born to please men, and Helen was one of these. Well educated, cultured, beautiful, she appeared out of place on the rough mountain, yet her quick brain and her instinct for making money kept her on the Comstock. And only the day before she had told him that trading in mining stocks was just a gambling game, a game he could learn as well as any other.

He still could not explain her interest in him. He worried over it when they were separated, but when he was with her everything else was crowded from his mind.

He finished his inspection of the bulkhead and headed for the face. There was no sound of drilling there, and as he came up, the crew on shift was clustered around the foreman, their cap lights bobbing, their voices high in argument. He judged it to be a crisis of some kind and pushed in to the man at the center.

"What's going on?"

The foreman looked uncertain. "They want to quit. The Savage just blew another shot, close." His eyes searched the rock roof anxiously. "They're going to break through on us any time now, and when they do, anybody up here is dead."

It was the old argument, the miners' fear that when the ceiling between the tunnel and the mine was breached the poison gasses from above would sink through the hole and, added to the tunnel's foul air, choke them. Murdock did not like the prospect himself, but he did have a growing confidence in Sutro.

"You know what the old man says. The gas will rise, not come down."

There was a general growl of disagreement. One miner said, "Why doesn't the bastard come down here himself then? Hell with it. I'm getting out." He started toward the tool room at the tunnel side.

"Nobody's going until the end of the shift." Murdock's voice was flat, hard.

There was a chorus. "Who's going to keep us from it?"

"I am."

One miner grabbed up a single jack and swung it suggestively. Murdock pulled his gun from its holster.

"The order is to rush the ditch through. Get about it."

For awhile they stood like hungry animals. They could rush him. He could not shoot them all even if he wanted to try. Casually he put his fingers to the healing scar on his cheek, a reminder of his fight with Boris Stucki. It worked. No one, it appeared, wanted to challenge this chief. The single jack clattered to the floor and the men turned sullenly back to work. Murdock continued to watch them, leaning against the rough wall, somehow feeling foolish.

At the end of the shift he followed them out and stopped in Bluett's office to report. Sheldon was there and they listened with troubled expressions.

Bluett swore. "It's ticklish, I know. They're all scared and you can't convince them. I don't know myself which way to believe. But that ditch has to be finished if you have to put a police detail over them with guns."

Sheldon said, "I hate to ask it, I know you're short of sleep, but we'd better tell Sutro to expect trouble. I'll write a note while you get ready."

Ken Murdock did not object to going up the hill. It would give him another chance to see Helen Powell.

Chapter Eight

There was little discussed in the bunkhouses that evening except the imminence of the Savage crew breaking through to the tunnel. It was frightened talk and there was talk of wholesale quitting. But they had more than two weeks of pay coming that they would lose if they walked off the job. It tended to hold them in spite of fear.

In the boarding house Sheila listened to the same talk around the supper table and afterward in the parlor, only half hearing. She was very conscious that Ken Murdock had come home earlier, changed his clothes and taken off for Virginia.

At eight she went to the kitchen to give the maids instructions before they left for the night. Al Temple found her there an hour later, sitting quietly at the worktable, a cup of cold coffee at her elbow. She looked up, met his eyes and managed a smile, then she rose, brought him a cup from the pot on the stove, emptied her own and refilled it and dropped back to her chair.

"Al, what do you think?"

He sat down, stretching his long legs tiredly. "About what?"

"The danger at the face when the Savage breaks through."

"Just pray they get that flume built first. The Savage may try to empty their sumps on us."

"I meant the gas."

"Sutro keeps insisting it's lighter than air, that it will go up through the mine. Let the Savage worry about it."

"Do you believe that?"

He wrinkled his nose and his lips twisted wryly. "All I'm sure of is it smells like hell in there now, and I mean *hell*. If the old man isn't right it will be murder."

"What are they going to do?"

"I don't know. Sheldon sent Murdock up to talk to Sutro, but my guess is he'll say pour on the coal until that flume is ready."

"So that's where Ken went. I wondered, when he didn't show up for supper."

Temple's mouth tightened, his voice turned gruff. "Where'd you think he went, to see the Powell woman?"

Her lashes dropped, veiling her eyes.

He leaned across the table suddenly, reaching for her hand. "Sheila—you know how I feel about you . . ."

"Don't, please." She drew back.

He drew a deep breath to steady his tone. "You're wasting your time on this Murdock, honey. Helen Powell is making a fool of him. She's smart. She's been mixed up with some of the biggest men in camp. She knows the score."

"Then what does she want with Ken?"

The words were wrenched from her. They told Temple more than he wanted to hear.

"What's she doing, just playing?"

Bitterness soured his voice. "If you ask me, she's stringing him along for what he can tell her."

"What could he tell that she'd want to hear?"

"About the tunnel. Sutro and Sheldon and Bluett have always been very careful who they let underground. Now suppose this Powell woman is trading in tunnel stock. Don't you think it would help her to know exactly how Sutro is making out with the mineowners, for instance?"

Her eyes came up, widening on him. "You mean Ken is spying? I don't believe it."

"No," Temple sounded disgusted. "He hasn't got sense enough to spy consciously. He's too green. He thinks the woman is taken with his pretty eyes and curly hair. He probably tells her everything that happens just to make out that he's a big man."

"Don't say that."

He looked at her for a long moment in silence, then he moved his shoulders, a small, hopeless gesture. "I guess you've got it bad."

She did not answer. He rose, leaned over the table and planted a light kiss on the top of her head.

"He isn't worth it. Not you, Sheila. Forget him."

She heard him leave the kitchen, climb the rear stairs, and sat on alone. She heard the front door open and glanced at the wall clock. It read three-thirty.

Her muscles were stiff from sitting as she got up and went through to the parlor. Ken Murdock was there, warming his hands against the cooling iron of the stove. His soft smile cut off as he saw her.

"Something the matter? What are you doing up?"

"I couldn't sleep." She said it truthfully. "Come in the kitchen, I'll give you some coffee."

He followed her gratefully, and in some surprise at her lack of hostility. She gave him not only coffee but a wedge of dried apple pie, then sat down across from him.

"Did you see Sutro?"

He nodded, swallowing.

"What does he say?"

"Push the ditch as hard as we can. The mine people threatened again to dump their water on us."

"They haven't signed then?"

Murdock shook his head.

"Do you think they ever will?"

"The old man insists they'll have to. Any day now."

She sat watching him finish the pie, then said suddenly, as if on impulse, "Don't go into the tunnel again."

He looked up, startled. "Don't go? That's my job. Sutro is depending on me."

She leaned toward him earnestly. "You don't owe him a

65

thing. What has he done for you? Sold his worthless stock to your brother—conned you along with his pipe dream . . ."

"Whoa up." There was shock in his voice. "I don't agree. Adolph Sutro isn't conning anyone."

"You say," she flashed at him. "The trouble with you is, you never know when you're being used. Ken, I don't want you hurt—I don't want you killed . . ."

He shook his head hard. "I'm not going to be. What's got into you?"

She was on her feet, her eyes sparking. "I might as well talk to a stone hitching post. You're the stubbornnest man alive. You let Sutro make a cat's-paw of you—you run after that Powell woman like a poodle dog on a string. Go ahead, get yourself gassed and boiled in hot water and see who cares." She ran out through the rear door and slammed it behind her.

Ken Murdock stared at the door. He sat there for a long time. When he finally went up to bed it was not to sleep.

Trouble flared again in the tunnel during the night when that shift revolted, and in the morning Murdock found Jack Bluett facing the changeover men, red-faced and shouting. They were flatly refusing to go beyond the bulkhead.

"I know it's uncomfortable up there," he argued. "So does Sutro, but that station has to be finished. Either you go in and work or you walk out now and you won't come back. I mean it. Make up your minds."

Some turned and went outside. The others watched them, considering what quitting meant. Everything on the Comstock was slow at the moment. Half the mines were working only one shift. If they lost their jobs in the tunnel the chances were slim that they could catch on anywhere else, and they had little money behind them to carry them over.

It was the foreman who finally capitulated. "Ah—hell." He scrubbed gnarled fingers through his bristly hair. The worry was stark in his eyes, but he shouldered through his crew, heading for the mule-drawn carts that would haul them to the face and slowly, reluctantly, his men followed him.

Bluett mopped his face with a red handkerchief. "It's getting rougher," he told Murdock. "You'd better stay up there with them all shift. They're liable to panic next time the Savage blasts."

Murdock rode alone in the last car, stopping to inspect the air vents, the hoses, the crew that was pushing the ditch forward. There was a lot of it incomplete, a lot more not even begun. And it could not be begun unless new funds came in. He could himself feel Bluett's, Sheldon's, Sutro's bitter frustration. If only the mines would sign, the whole project could be finished and doing the job that was so desperately needed.

By the time he reached the face the crew was busy but jittery, stopping for ice and rest every few minutes. A squabble started that he had to break up with the threat of his gun. Then things went smoothly for an hour and he leaned against the rock wall, the heat and his lack of sleep making him dopey.

A yell, then a chorus of them brought him alert, but it took him a minute to find the cause. Two feet of a steel drill protruded down through the ceiling, wobbling as it continued to spin against the air. The workmen were frozen, staring up openmouthed as if at a visitor from another planet.

"God." It was the foreman's cry. "They've broke through . . ."

One man dropped his hammer, shouting, "I'm getting the hell out of here before the gas comes down."

There was a rush of panic, men running, bumping against each other in the hurry to get away from the face. Ken Murdock came fully awake then, drew his gun and blocked the exit with his big body.

"Stop it. Stand still. I'll shoot the first man who tries to pass me."

They stopped, glaring at him in desperation. The foreman yelled.

"We've got to get out, before they pull the bit, before the gas comes down."

"Use your head," he yelled back. "Not enough can come through that size hole to hurt you right away. If it comes we'll move past the bulkhead and close it. Just wait."

He saw the strain in their faces, their eyes. He saw the way their hands tightened on the hammers and knew that within seconds they would rush him. He might shoot one or two, but not all. He risked a glance at the ceiling.

The bit was being pulled, leaving a hole through which

foul air would draw, one way or the other. Then a flicker of light pulled his attention down and he shouted, "It's all right. It's going up. Look at your lamps."

The flames of the head lamps were bending backward, toward the opening.

It took a moment for his words to penetrate their concentration on escape, then they looked at each other, at the lamps. The foreman spun and ran, licking his forefinger, thrusting it up into the hole, his sweated face tight. Then he pulled the finger out and said in a shaking voice, "It's going up. Come here, feel it."

A second man joined him like a sleepwalker, then a third, then the crew clustered under the hole taking turns, shoving their fingers into the hole, feeling the draft of the rising air, their disbelief finally giving way to relief.

Murdock dropped his gun back to its holster. He felt washed out. He had come within an ace of shooting one man, perhaps more, of being beaten to the ground, killed by hammers swung by these powerfully muscled men. In their fear and panic there would have been no quarter.

Now they were laughing, pounding each other on the back. For weeks they had worked in dread of being smothered, poisoned. It was not that they lacked ordinary courage. Any man working underground needed courage. It was the unknown that had held them in a stranglehold. And now they had their proof that Sutro was right, and he was their idol again.

Murdock left quietly. They would finish the shift now without any threat from him. He hurried back to the tunnel entrance and ran to Sheldon's office, found Bluett there and broke the news to both men. While he caught his breath they looked at each other, silent, each in his mind seeing back over the uncertain years. Then Sheldon jumped for the telegraph instrument. Again the perverse machine was dead. Sheldon turned back, irony twisting his mouth.

"I guess it's you again, Ken. Sutro has to hear as soon as possible. Don't wait to change clothes. Go get your coat and I'll order a horse."

He swung out of the door. Murdock waited only long enough to speak the words that were crowding up through him, more to himself than to Bluett.

"Adolph Sutro. That's a great man, Jack."

"The greatest. Any ordinary man would have quit years ago. Hadn't you better be moving?"

Ken ran, got his coat and met Sheldon leading the saddled horse toward him from the livery.

The animal was fresh and wanted to run. Ken let it out on the level trail to Dayton. An exhilaration filled him. It was good to be in a saddle again, to be riding through clear air in the sunshine, to be out from underground. The quicker the tunnel was finished and he could get back to his ranch the better he would like it.

The only thing that troubled him now was Helen Powell. He could not visualize her as a ranch wife, carrying wood from the shed, water from the well, helping to feed the stock, doing her washing in a tin tub with water heated on the stove.

He tried to put the problem away from him. This was a time for celebration, not for worry. But the conflict of his love of the ranch and his want of her nagged him. He was sure that he could never be happy without both of them.

The climb up the steep grade through Gold Hill, where the horse could do no more than walk, was painfully slow. Then he was over the divide, dodging among the crawling freight wagons and carriages to the livery.

Sutro was in his room working at a pile of papers that littered his desk. His eyes were bright, lively, exultant as he listened, then in surprise Murdock saw his face cloud.

"What time did they break through?"

"About eleven o'clock."

Sutro stood up, looking at his watch, hurrying toward the door.

"Come on, son."

Murdock followed him from the hotel and down the street to the Savage mine. A clerk tried to stop them as Sutro stalked in. Sutro shoved him aside and plowed on into the mine superintendent's office.

Gillette looked up, his eyes widening, then he came to his feet, frowning. "Sutro. What are you doing here?"

Sutro said without greeting, "One of your drills came through the tunnel roof this morning. The telegraph is out so

I can't order the hole plugged. Get it blocked right away, before our accumulated gasses seep into your mine."

Gillette was blank-faced for a moment, then he laughed, a sound with no humor. "Let your crew look out for our gas, Adolph. I don't subscribe to your theory that it will rise."

"It is rising. Your miners on the lower levels can be asphyxiated."

Gillette's smile was cold. "They can take their chances."

"Also, don't let them enlarge that hole. Our drainage flume isn't ready yet."

The cold smile widened. "That, my dear man, is your problem, not mine."

Murdock saw the muscles in Sutro's heavy shoulders bunch. It was the only indication of an inner rage, and there was no change in his tone of voice.

"Mr. Gillette," he used the formal address caustically. "If you let so much as a drop of water from your sumps into that tunnel you're in trouble. We have a watertight bulkhead which we will close. Your water will back up behind it and flood your lower workings."

He flicked a finger at Murdock and with Ken trailing him, strode out of the office.

Chapter Nine

On the street Sutro stopped and stood in stolid anger. He blew out his breath so hard that his side whiskers bounced.

"The dunderhead."

He was too wrought up to say more at the moment, puffing noisily until he could control himself. Then he thundered. "I've got to stop them. If the damn fools load that drill hole and blow out the tunnel roof, every man down there can be killed."

He wheeled back into the office. Again the clerk tried to intercept him. Sutro barked at Murdock, "If he doesn't get out of our way, knock him down."

The clerk was a small man past middle age. He looked at Murdock's expressionless face and scurried around his high desk, and they passed him. But Gillette had already gone down into the mine.

They moved on to the three-compartmented shaft that connected the surface with the bowels of the mine. Sutro signaled for the lift and a square cage, its sides fenced with wire, shot up, the door slid open. Sutro moved to step inside and was barred by the liftman.

"Nobody goes down. Boss's orders."

Sutro spoke without looking at Murdock. "Tell the man we're going down."

For a moment Murdock did not understand. They were on Savage property, they had no authority here, and the orders were Gillette's.

Sutro spoke again, softly. "You have a gun. Tell him."

Murdock lifted the gun from its holster, held it loosely, aimed at the floor, saw the man's shocked face.

"Mr. Sutro wants to go down."

Guardedly the man stepped out of the way. Murdock followed Sutro into the cage and the door clanged shut. The lift dropped with a suddenness that made Murdock's stomach seem to turn and leap up into his throat.

They passed level after level, falling so fast that Murdock had only a sensation of flashing lights. Then the cage bounced to a stop at a station and a crowd of men there turned to stare in amazement.

Gillette saw them come out of the cage and pushed forward, flushing with anger.

"You—I gave orders to keep all outsiders out of here . . ."

Sutro cut him short. "There isn't time to argue. Don't enlarge that hole."

Gillette sneered. "Sorry. Shots are already set. They'll blow any . . ."

The station rocked suddenly with the force of the blast. The next instant those in the mine drift were driven back into the station by a roiling of noxious gasses sweeping up from the tunnel.

They came in panic, stumbling, choking, coughing, their eyes streaming from the burning gas that doubled the foulness of the air they normally breathed. Some fell in collapse as they reached the station.

Gillette, one of the most experienced superintendents on the Lode, abandoned his anger at Sutro and threw himself into the job of bringing order, physically fighting his miners away from the cage as they threatened to overload it in the frenzied scramble for safety.

The two tunnel men were forgotten. Sutro clapped a handkerchief over his mouth and nose, caught Murdock's arm, said a muffled, "Hold your breath," and towed Ken at a run down the drift.

A faint light showed ahead, glowing up from the gaping hole blown by the blast. Murdock thought Sutro had lost his mind as he rushed into the dense fumes. Then, as they neared the breakthrough, the poisonous air bettered. The tunnel blowers were forcing cleaner air against the face, pushing the concentrated combination before it.

At the edge of the break they found that the dynamite had caved the floor of the Savage drift, dropped a section five foot across into the tunnel below. Light and excited voices came up to them.

Sutro sat down on the ragged lip and eased his bulk through the opening. Murdock came right behind him. A six-foot drop landed them on the heap of shattered rubble. Murdock saw the men of the shift crowded back against the walls and unconsciously counted them. Miraculously they were all there, all standing. None had been caught under the falling ceiling. For a moment they gaped at the two apparitions, then the foreman found his wits and jumped to help Sutro out of the debris.

They gathered around him with a babble of questions. Sutro only stood, not answering. Looking at him, Murdock saw the man was crying, unable to speak. A flash of insight told him what this instant meant to the tunnel builder. After the years of struggle, recurring failures, of stubbornly held hope that had been dashed again and again by his enemies, Sutro was vindicated. The dream was a reality. The tunnel at last had reached the Comstock Lode. A connection was made.

All of the mines along the monster ore body were interwoven underground. For years their workings had broken through into each other. But they could not be served by this single umbilicus. North and south arms still needed to be dug at right angles to the main tunnel, opening into each mine, but that should come quickly now that the theory of rising air was proven. It was already cleaner in the tunnel than Murdock had ever known it.

Slowly, as if dazed, Sutro began moving toward an empty ore car, and climbed into it. As Murdock shoved after him through the ring of men he saw Al Temple and two tunnel police standing at the mouth of the station. They had, he guessed, run up from the bulkhead at the sound of the blast. He beckoned Al to him and when they met at the side of the car, told him, "Stay up here and watch close. The Savage may try to come through to get at the bulkhead."

Then he climbed into the car and rode with Sutro toward the distant entrance. Word of the breakthrough had run before them. They were cheered all along the way and at the Sutro end there was a wild scene. Jack Bluett, Sheldon and Sutro acted like three excited kids, laughing, dancing, punching at each other.

Murdock stood aside, feeling out of it. He was not one of the officers, had no participation in the accomplishment. In part he appreciated it, but his main reaction was that now the mines would have to sign and the tunnel stock would climb. He could recover his money, return to Oregon, buy back his ranch—and then he thought of Helen Powell, and for the first time considered that he might not go home to Oregon.

His mind came back to the tunnel office. Sutro was assuring Sheldon that it was now only a matter of days, perhaps hours before the mineowners would line up to sign his contracts, that their troubles were nearly over.

"It calls for a celebration, does it not? I'll tell you what we'll do. I'll get my children, then we'll all go up to Virginia and dine at the French restaurant. But this time we will not go by road. We will go by the tunnel and up through the Savage mine."

Bluett objected. "Maybe Gillette won't let us use the mine. Besides, the air is too bad for people not used to it."

"It's clearing. It's already better than it's ever been. That is one advantage of the tunnel that has not been emphasized.

The mine shafts will be ventilated as they never have been before." He was thoughtful for a moment, then he turned to Murdock.

"You come with us and bring another man on whom you can depend, just in case we do meet a resistance from the Savage people."

Murdock said, "When do you want to go?"

Sutro studied his heavy gold hunter's case watch. "Let's start in two hours." He put the watch away and suddenly spread his arms wide, expansively, to Sheldon and Bluett. "Go round up all the officials of the miners' union and the county officers who have stood by us. This shall be a real victory banquet."

Murdock thought first of Al Temple, already inside, then changed his mind. The bulkhead needed protection now more than ever. He headed for the bunkhouse, running lightly, dashing through the door, caught up in the buoyant mood of the office. Sheila was passing through the front room. She stopped and pressed her hand against her mouth.

"What's happened now?"

He pulled up short and grinned at her. "The Savage broke through."

"I know that—it's all over town . . ."

"I don't mean the drill." His excitement grew as he talked. "They blasted through. A hole five feet across."

She gasped. "And the gas?"

He laughed aloud. "Went up just like old Sutro said it would. The man's a genius. You ought to see him. He's won. He's beat the whole Comstock."

"The mines have signed?"

"They will now. They'll have to. Is Stucki here?"

"Asleep."

He ran up the stairs and burst into the Russian's room.

The man was snoring. Even the noise of Murdock's entrance did not rouse him. Murdock caught the covers and yanked them off the bulky body.

"Shake it up, man. Come along."

Stucki opened his eyes groggily, angrily. "What the hell . . . ?"

"We've got an escort job." He ran through a quick briefing

74

of the events and the mission. "Get your clothes on. There'll be free champagne tonight for everybody if I know Sutro."

Stucki swung his big feet off the bed. In his thick underwear he looked like a ruffled bear. As Murdock's words drove the sleep from his mind his grin spread.

"You think there'll be trouble?" He reached for his pants, sounding eager.

"How do I know?" Ken Murdock hoped that there would not be.

They met the Sutro party outside the tunnel office: Sutro's two daughters Kate and Clara, his sons Charles and Edgar; Jo Aron, an old friend of Sutro's whose banking connections in New York had made the tunnel possible; the publisher of the local paper and other dignitaries. Murdock knew most of the local men by sight but he had not seen Sutro's family before. All of them were bundled into a hurriedly collected assortment of outer clothing over their town wear against the dirt of the coming sortie. They trailed into the tunnel and boarded the mule-drawn passenger cars waiting there, and for the first time laughter and singing echoed down the four-mile corridor as the gala gathering progressed.

Murdock and Stucki, ahead, paused at the bulkhead and heard from Al Temple that no one from the Savage had tried to come down. At the face a ladder had been propped against the rim of the hole. Murdock climbed the rungs until his head thrust into the Savage drift. And there he stopped.

He had been relaxed by Temple's news. Now tension coiled in him. He was eye level with a pair of widespread booted feet. He looked up, aware of other feet behind these, looked into the muzzle of a gun aimed at his head, looked higher and found Buck Shaw's brutal face grinning down at him.

It was a shock to both of them. Then Shaw recovered and motioned with his gun.

"Back down, bucko. Nobody's coming up here."

Murdock wanted no trouble here, with the festive party coming close behind him. He kept his voice level, conciliatory.

"Mr. Sutro has a whole bunch of friends here, plus his children. All they want is to use the Savage lift to go up for a celebration in town. It won't hurt the mine. Call Mr. Gillette. I'm sure he'll give permission."

Shaw laughed. "Think again, mister. Gillette told me plain. Crazy Adolph nor any of his crowd is ever to step foot on Savage property again. That goes personally for you. Back off before I blow your head apart."

Below Murdock, Sutro was pacing impatiently. Murdock felt a tug at his leg and the tunnel man called up.

"Get out of the way, boy. Let me talk to him."

Carefully Murdock climbed down and watched uneasily as Sutro went up. Beside him at the bottom Stucki growled hungrily.

"I'd like a shot at those bastards."

"Not with the kids here."

"We going to just stand here and let him make jackasses out of us?"

"Maybe not. Wait awhile. Be ready to cover me." He turned to the crowd, unobtrusively easing it back into the station, away from the hole. Then he returned to the side of the ladder. In the dim light no one could see that he drew his gun. All attention was on Sutro, arguing with Shaw, saying, "Get hold of Gillette. Tell him if we aren't allowed to pass through the mine I'll wire the head of the Savage board in San Francisco."

Shaw's harsh laugh came down. "Adolph, when are you going to get some sense through that thick German head? The order to keep you out came directly from San Francisco. Gillette already wired for instructions. The answer was that any of you who tried to come up through this hole should get shot. That's it. So get out of here."

Sutro swore softly under his breath and slowly backed down. Murdock winked at Stucki and as Sutro left the bottom rung brushed past him and silently, swiftly climbed, thrusting the nose of his gun ahead of him over the rim. Shaw had already dropped his gun back to its holster, was turning to the men behind him, laughing. His big body blocked them from seeing Murdock.

Murdock eased high enough to see Shaw and raised his aim to the man's middle.

"Buck," he said quietly, "don't reach for the gun again. Just unbuckle your belt and let it slide."

The mine policeman's head snapped around. Quick anger wiped away his laugh. "Mister," he said, "you've asked for it before. This time I'll have to kill you."

"Maybe later." Murdock still spoke softly. "Right now, if you go for that gun you're a dead man. Unbuckle that belt."

For a long-drawn instant it seemed to Murdock that the man would defy him, and wondered if he could shoot him down in cold blood. And then Shaw made his decision, slowly lifting his left hand to the buckle, loosening it, letting the belt and holstered gun slide to the stone floor.

Murdock moved up a rung, bringing his head and shoulders above the drift level. "Now tell your men to drop theirs. If any one of them tries anything, you get shot in the stomach."

Shaw was so bloated with anger that he could barely speak, but without looking behind him he nodded. There were four mine police with him, men long used to lording it over the Lode. They liked this no better than Buck Shaw did. But they saw little choice. Not one doubted that Ken Murdock would fire. Their guns clanked down on the rock at their feet.

Murdock shifted to the side of the ladder, calling down to Stucki without turning his head. "Climb past me and pick up the guns, then back the men to the station. Hold them there until I get Sutro's party onto the lift."

The Russian came up, grinning widely. This was the way he liked it, having the drop on the mine police who had given him trouble in the past. His gun in his hand, he climbed out of the hole like a giant spider, careful not to move his thick body between Murdock's gun and Buck Shaw.

"Move off four steps, then stand still," he said, and, his eyes bright on the group, kicked the belts one by one down through the hole.

Murdock called to a workman below to throw the belts and guns into one of the cars and watched Stucki march his captives down the drift backward, stalking them like a preying cat. Then he beckoned the party up.

Sutro came first, reaching for the hand Murdock extended to help him up, pressing it, saying with a sly grin, "I won't forget this, Ken."

It was the first time Sutro had used his given name and it

sent a warmth through Murdock as he helped the children one at a time through the hole. He crowded the surge down. By this time he knew Sutro's history well, the many broken promises interspersed through the kindnesses and the enormous feats. Still, the warmth outweighed the doubt.

He ushered the party along the drift to the station and rang the clamoring bell for the lift. Stucki had Shaw's men grouped against the far wall of the station and as the lift plummeted down and jounced to a stop, the operator saw them, saw Sutro's crowd. His eyes bugged. He tried to close the gate.

"What the hell . . . ?"

Murdock had learned his lesson. He knew now that the only rules that held underground were those backed up by force. He showed his gun.

"Mr. Sutro and his friends want to go to the surface."

He motioned the Sutro party into the big, square cage, followed them, then called to Stucki to join them.

Stucki backed to the cage, his gun still covering the police. "Have fun, boys," he laughed at them. "Next time I see you I'll shoot first and listen to your beefs later." He stepped through the gate, heard it close and laughed again at the curses that followed him as Murdock signaled the operator and the cage shot up.

In the mine's change room above, the party shucked out of the rough overclothing, then Sutro led them in a parade down C Street to the French Rotisserie.

Murdock and Stucki kept alert for any interference on the street, but there was only open curiosity from the people they passed. The story of the breakthrough was already spread across the Lode. Now the men were making bets on what the mineowners would do.

At the restaurant Sutro caught Murdock's arm in a friendly vise. "I'd like to ask you to join us," he said, "but I want to make certain no one interrupts our celebration. Will you stay beside the door and see that we are not disturbed?"

Murdock nodded, pleased with the development, waited until the door closed behind the parade, then spoke to Stucki, an unconscious lift in his voice.

"Boris, I've got a little business down the street—it will take maybe half an hour. Watch for . . ."

"Just one minute," Stucki cut in. "What about that champagne you promised me?"

Murdock's impatience rode him. "You can wait half an hour, can't you?"

Stucki sounded suspicious. "Whenever—who's going to pay for it? I thought you said Sutro would."

Murdock had thought so too. He said quickly, "I'll buy. As much as you can pour into that hogshead you call a carcass. As soon as this duty is over. I'll be back way before then."

The Russian snorted. "You're in a real sweat. You going to see that Powell woman?"

Murdock flushed hotly. "It's none of your damn business where I'm going."

Stucki caught his shoulder in one big hand. "Look, bucko, just because you licked me once don't say you're smarter than me. That woman isn't for the likes of you or me. She's money hungry, that's what she is, and she's got half the owners and superintendents on her list."

He swung Ken away as Murdock's fists balled. "Don't start a fight here. Crazy Adolph wouldn't like that. I'm just trying to get you to wise up to yourself. Women are poison for any man and that one worse than most. But go ahead, hang yourself. It's none of my affair."

Chapter Ten

Helen Powell was honestly very glad to see him. The exchange had closed some time ago and except for her the customers' room was empty.

She was at her desk going over columns of figures. Under the soft light of the student lamp Ken Murdock found her the most desirable creature he had ever seen.

She looked up and he searched her face for trace of the greed of which Stucki had accused her. He found nothing but reassurement there. Her eyes lighted and she rose in one single graceful, rhythmic gesture.

"Ken. How nice. Why didn't you let me know you'd be in town? I have a dinner date later—a business date."

"I didn't know I'd be coming," he said. "Anyhow, I can only stay a few minutes. This has been a pretty busy day."

Her brows arched, asking her unspoken question. He came to the desk and she looked up at him for a long, silent moment, then motioned him into a chair and said eagerly, "Tell me."

He sank down to the seat with a deep pleasure at her undisguised interest. "You must have heard about the Savage breaking through into the tunnel?"

"Rumors." She shrugged prettily. "The town's buzzed all afternoon but nobody knows exactly what happened. Gillette won't talk, Sutro's vanished. I've been in telegraph contact with our correspondents in San Francisco and none of the Savage people there will talk either."

He grinned at her. "I was there at the time the drill first came through. It was a bad minute." He told her about the workmen's fright, their near mutiny before the gas began to rise as Sutro had predicted.

Her eyes glinted and she laughed at the story of Gillette trying to keep them out of the mine and their forcing their way in. She gasped when he told how the Savage had blown the hole, and when he described the parade from Sutro to the surface through the Savage she rested a small hand over his on the chair arm. The touch of her fingers was electric. It set his pulse hammering. Her voice was rich, warm.

"I hope Sutro appreciates all the help you've given him. What does he think about the mines signing now?"

"He's sure they will."

She drew a long, careful breath. She had been on tenterhooks all day. The tunnel stocks had bounced up and down like a rubber ball with each succeeding rumor, but no one on the exchange knew for certain what was taking place underground because the Savage management had been able to keep the brokers' spies out of the lower workings. Now she was talking to a man who had witnessed it all. Her tone was cautious.

"Is that your guess or what Adolph thinks?"

He laughed. "What Adolph thinks. I wouldn't know anything about it."

She pressed him. "He said that?"

He nodded.

Behind her admiring smile her mind was busy. In her view Adolph Sutro was one of the smartest men on the Comstock, though she never said so aloud. He had forced the tunnel forward against the opposition of the powerful Bank of California, of the Bonanza Kings, of all the mining interests that controlled the Comstock. In the face of their combined obstructions he had raised money from the United States government, from the Lazard Frères of Paris and the McCalmonts.

She patted Murdock's hand lightly, then reached for the delicate watch suspended from a gold chain pinned to her dress.

"It's fascinating to listen to you, Ken, and I'm sorry that I can't stay. But I'm late now."

He rose with her, knowing a keen disappointment. It was the same every time they separated. He tried to keep it out of his voice.

"I don't know when I'll get the chance to see you again."

"You will."

She caught his hand again in both of her own, squeezing it. Suddenly, as if on an irresistible impulse, she raised onto her toes and lifted her mouth up to his.

For an instant he was too startled to take advantage of her offer, then he pulled her against him, made rough by his rush of desire, and crushed his mouth against hers. She pressed to him for a moment, then gently pushed him away.

"Please."

He started to murmur that he was sorry but she cut him short.

"These things happen." Her tone was soft.

"But I . . ."

She laid her fingers against his lips. "Ken, not now. I'm very late. You can walk with me to the hotel if you like."

"Gladly." He held her cloak and moved at her side down C Street toward the International.

At the door she offered her hand. "Good night. Come to see me whenever you get to town." Then she was gone, with a light, tripping step across the lobby toward the elevators.

He watched her out of sight, then headed back for the restaurant in a dazed dream.

Helen Powell did not look back nor think back, her mind running ahead to the meeting that had been called in her uncle's rooms. She rode the elevator up and hurried down the corridor to the doors at the end.

Henry Powell let her into the living room, searching her eyes. Four men were already there, seated around a polished table, the air above their heads blue with cigar smoke. They rose automatically, waited as she put her cloak aside and took the chair her uncle held for her, then sat again. Henry Powell spoke as he took the chair at the head of the table.

"Did he come?"

She nodded briefly, her eyes bright. "And it was worth waiting for." She repeated in detail everything Murdock had told her.

There was no immediate visible reaction. The men took time, weighing the implications. It was her uncle who finally spoke.

"So the connection was made in the early afternoon. Yet we know that none of the mines has signed as of an hour ago."

"They will." Helen Powell sounded certain. "Sutro has survived against everyone so far. And now the connection has proved it will ventilate the mines and can get rid of the water, the heat. The miners' union will start pressuring the companies for relief. The men are fed up with the conditions they're working under, gas, heat, the danger of fire. They'll force the signings. For my part I say we go ahead. Each of us put up a hundred thousand dollars. That will give our syndicate nine hundred thousand in the trading account."

She looked at each man, judging their readiness, then went on, taking the lead as if it were her right, and no one challenged her.

"We'll send Dick Ross to San Francisco where he can work without rousing the suspicion he would here. Buy on margin, carefully, so the price isn't forced up. With a kitty that size we should be able to control at least five million shares."

She smiled at Ross, a chunky man with reddish, curling

hair, a man known as one of the major specialists in the business. The man shook his head.

"We'd raise the market a dozen points. There isn't that much stock floating in San Francisco."

"But there is in New York, London, Paris. A lot of the foreign bankers have already written off the tunnel as a bad investment. While you work through the New York offices we'll concentrate on the miners. Everybody in Virginia has a few hundred shares. We can't miss."

She saw Ross gradually agree and the others follow.

Ross said, "How long do you think we have?"

"Not more than thirty days. Less if the mines capitulate all at once. You'd better catch the midnight train, Dick. Use three or four brokers. Don't tell them more than you have to. Let them think you're executing orders for individuals. Don't buy more than two hundred shares at any one price. If it goes too high, sell enough to one of us to break it back."

They bent over the table, debating, refining plans until Ross had to leave to catch his train. When they had gone, Henry Powell smiled at his niece.

"It looks very pretty, Helen. We might start by taking your young friend Murdock's stock off his hands."

"Oh, no you don't," she said quickly. "Do that and when the rise comes he'll think we cheated him. Then where do we get our information? Let him alone while we need him."

She rose then and retired to her own room. In that sanctuary she gave over to being pleased with herself. When this was finished she should come out with better than a million dollars. And how fast she would leave this mountain, head for New York and perhaps London or Paris. She would wash out all memory of this grubby mining camp. To the men she had used, was using, she gave no thought, least of all to Ken Murdock.

But Ken Murdock was thinking of her, seeing her as a transparent vision between his eyes and the people before him.

He had given Stucki a ten-dollar gold piece, knowing that the man would be roaring drunk within the hour, then he had taken up a position from which he could watch both the entrance and the Sutro celebration. But what he saw and heard were less real to him than his vision.

Adolph was a bouncing host, on his feet again and again proposing toasts as the dinner ran its course, and at last, with his children nodding in exhaustion, he offered one final salute.

"To our imminent success, good friends. To the capitulation of the mines and all others who have fought us so long. Within very few days our contracts will be signed and all of our troubles past."

Chapter Eleven

As he had been many times before, Adolph Sutro was too optimistic. And Helen Powell's time estimate was too short. The mineowners continued to hold out. Spring dragged into summer and summer into fall. Then winter was on them again and still no contracts were signed.

Work within the tunnel went on as if the breakthrough had never occured. Sutro doggedly continued his negotiations. He also found time to promote the branch tunnels which would make connection with the other mines along the Lode and to press the enclosed ditch that would drain out the waters.

Working conditions were a little more bearable with the ventilation through the Savage, but it was still slow. The ditch was far from finished, its progress hampered as always by a shortage of money. To find funds now, Sutro resorted to an issue of more treasury stock.

It was that issue that broke Helen Powell and her syndicate which had been amassing the stock on margin.

As the weeks passed and brought no announcement of any mine contracting with the tunnel, the Powell people had grown uneasy, then more and more desperate.

In the beginning of their operations everything had gone according to their plan. They had been able to buy without boosting the price of the sluggish stock above what they considered a danger point, although it had now nearly tripled from the time they began to buy.

Sutro and his aides had watched the steady rise, poised for

their move. Certificates that had gone begging with no takers at any price were now selling at three dollars. It was at that level when he threw a hundred thousand extra shares on the market.

The stock broke dramatically. On Wednesday morning it sold at three-twenty asked. At the close of the market Wednesday night it was refused at fifty cents.

It was a black and hectic day for Helen Powell. Through the careful months her syndicate had bought and sold and kept the market in intentional control. Their aim was to maneuver the price to five dollars and then unload simultaneously on all of the exchanges.

She had been disappointed when none of the mines had signed to help the stock rise quickly, but she had not worried, for the European bankers who had been Sutro's principal backers showed no inclination to dump their enormous holdings. And Murdock had reported to her week by week on Sutro's continuing confidence that agreement was coming soon.

Then on Wednesday morning blocks of stock were mysteriously offered on the Virginia exchange in unexpected quantities. Her floor men picked them up to maintain the price. But the more they bought the more was offered. By eleven o'clock the margin squeeze was tightening dangerously.

In a kind of panic she had never experienced before, Helen Powell wired Ken Murdock to contact her at once.

Murdock was sleeping after being up all night filling Stucki's shift. The Russian had gone on a three-day drunk. Jack Bryan brought the message when it was delivered from the local telegraph office. Murdock read:

Come to my office at once. Imperative I see you.

The ominous note drove the bleariness from his head. He threw his clothes on, ran to the barn and borrowed the fastest horse there. The trip up the mountain cost him two hours. It was after one o'clock when he hurried into the brokerage office.

It was a scene of confusion such as he had never seen there, of clerks rushing in and out with messages between the exchange and other brokers. The break in the tunnel stock had triggered a panic all across the board. Savage had dropped eleven points, Hale and Norcross was down eight and the mighty Con Virginia twenty.

Murdock shoved through the milling customers, pushed open the door of Helen Powell's private office and stopped in the entrance, breathless. The girl sagged at her desk, the latest report thrust at her by a clerk trembling in her hand. She lifted her eyes, saw Murdock, and said in a voice he hardly recognized. "Close the door. Come here."

He closed it, shutting out some of the turmoil of the outer room, searching the white, drawn face.

"What is it? What's wrong?"

"That's why I sent for you. To tell me. The bottom has fallen out of the market and the tunnel stock is leading the way."

He gaped at her, missing her meaning in his first reaction, the thought of what this would mean to Sutro's work.

"Oh, no."

"Oh, yes. It's down to fifty cents from a three-dollar opening. Why?"

Again he misinterpreted the question, shaking his head, saying, "There goes the chance to finish the drainage ditch, just when Sutro thought he had the money."

Her knuckles whitened on the desk edge as she lifted out of her chair. "Answer me. What is he doing?"

"Why, issuing a hundred thousand shares of new stock. They were about out of money and when the value went up . . ."

"When?" She snapped at him.

"This morning, I guess. I heard Sutro and Sheldon talking about it yesterday and . . ."

Her voice had been hoarse, hard to understand. It came up now, almost screeching. "And you didn't warn me—you fool." She reached for a silver bell and shook it, hard.

He stood befuddled, not understanding. The clerk rushing in all but knocked him down. The girl slammed her fist on the desk, slammed her words at the clerk.

"Sell. Tell them to sell. Send my uncle in here. Quick."

Murdock was left ignored as she waited, her eyes riveted on the door. When Henry Powell barged through it, she gasped bitterly. "It's what I guessed. Sutro's selling treasury stock. That's where it came from. That's what we've been buying all morning. This idiot knew and didn't tell us."

Her uncle went white, tumbled out a curse, then spun out of the room. The girl dropped into her chair and buried her face in her hands. An icy wave went through Murdock as he saw that she was crying.

He went to her quickly, put his hand on her shoulder. "Helen . . ."

She slapped the hand away. "Get out of here. Damn you."

He stood frozen, as if she had hit him in the face. His bewilderment made his voice climb sharply.

"What have I done?"

"Ruined us. Ruined all of us. Go . . ."

"But I don't understand."

"Of course you don't, you—you farmer. Get out. Leave me alone. Don't come back." She was talking through her hands, not even looking at him.

He went, stunned, carried along roughly by the crowd that was now erupting from the brokerage office. On the street he looked around him with the same lost feeling he had had the day he arrived but made worse by the girl's bitter outburst. Then he turned blindly toward the Crystal Palace.

He seldom took a drink in daytime, seldom took a drink alone, but he was so shaken that he needed the help of whiskey. The room was even fuller than usual. He crowded in against the bar between two miners, ordered as the bartender flicked by.

He was too deeply engrossed in his confusion about Helen to notice Buck Shaw come through the door with a pair of mine police. They stopped there, then at a motion from Shaw the three backed out.

Murdock had his drink, neat and quick. He had a second and debated a third, but unless Stucki showed up sober he would have to work that night again and he had no idea where the big Russian was.

He rang a dollar on the bar and shouldered out and started toward the hitch rail where he had left the horse. Before he reached the corner, Buck Shaw stepped suddenly out of a store doorway to face him.

Murdock stopped short. Shaw watched him, a mocking

smile twisting his thin-lipped mouth, his hand resting on the gun at his hip.

In his haste to answer the telegram from Helen he had neglected to put on his own belt.

The sidewalk was busy with hurrying men but none of them paid the slightest attention. If they had, no one would have interfered. A man was expected to take care of himself in Virginia.

From the corner of his eyes Murdock saw the two police move up on either side of him, and knew with a jolt that this meeting was no accident, that he was deliberately boxed.

He waited, the hot taste of fear in his mouth. He held no illusion that Shaw would hesitate to kill him. He had blocked the man twice, and neither time would be forgiven.

Shaw chuckled. "Well, sport, you picked a bad time to come to town."

He did not answer. There was nothing to say.

"Let's take a walk."

He almost refused. If they wanted to kill him he might as well die on C Street. Then he saw that one of the police carried a short club, saw him flex it and guessed that refusal would only earn him a cracked skull. And if he went, they might be content with giving him a beating. He nodded.

The pair closed in, caught his arms and turned him toward the buildings of the Savage mine. That suggested that they intended taking him down to the lower workings, killing him there, perhaps throwing his body through the connecting hole into the tunnel as an answer to Sutro's parade through the mine.

They crossed the street, dodging between ore wagons. On the far side a familiar voice called his name. They stopped, swinging around, hauling him with them. Stucki was a few feet away. Stucki was obviously drunk, rolling with every step, keeping a precarious balance.

"Hey, Murdock. Come have a drink."

Shaw's voice grated. "Shove off, you Russian bum."

Stucki halted, blinked, pouted. He was not wearing a gun belt.

Murdock said, "You'd better go on, Boris." He saw no reason for Stucki to get hurt.

"What's the matter?" The Russian stumbled and nearly

88

fell. "Too good to talk to me? Too good to have a drink with old Boris?"

He turned away as if to veer back across the crowded road. As he turned, his huge arm swept out and caught the man on Murdock's right along the side of his neck. The man fell down. And Stucki was jumping at Buck Shaw, his knees doubled up, hurtling into the mine policeman's stomach, driving him to the ground.

The man on Murdock's left was caught off guard. He dropped Murdock's arm and went for his gun.

Murdock swung a looping fist that hit the jaw so hard it sent pain racing up his forearm. The man crumpled and the gun slid from his nerveless fingers.

Murdock scooped it up, spinning, and was in time to see Stucki climb to his feet. The three on the ground did not move. The Russian grinned down on them. He was no longer drunk. Murdock realized now that he had not been drunk in the first place.

"Lucky you happened along. Thanks." He thrust the gun under his belt.

"No luck about it. Saw you come out of the Palace and was just about to hail you when I saw these coyotes move in. If I'd just had my iron I wouldn't have needed the drunk act."

"It's a good act that works. And I appreciate it."

Stucki grinned widely. "I ain't forgot that you licked me, bucko. Don't want anything to happen to you before I get the chance to even things. Now let's go get that drink."

Murdock did not want more whiskey but under the circumstance he could not say no. They went back to the Palace.

At midnight it suddenly occurred to him that one of them should be at the tunnel. He could not say where the evening had gone. He remembered that they had eaten a supper somewhere and he knew that he had had too much liquor. And by this time Stucki was not fooling. He was as drunk as he had pretended earlier.

He steered the big man to the patient horse, then led the animal on to the livery. Stucki could not recall where he had left his own mount. Murdock rented a buggy and needed the hostler's help to get the Russian up to the seat. Stucki immediately went to sleep.

Murdock was groggy, but somehow he got the rig through the Devil's Gate and down the grade. Somewhere along the road sleep overtook him and when the cold roused him the horse had come to a standstill in the middle of Dayton's main street. He shook the animal up and drove on.

He had to have help again, from one of the barn men, to wrestle the rubber-legged Stucki into the boarding house. When they pushed the door open they found Sheila Bryan dozing beside the stove.

She came awake and followed as they worked the Russian up the stairs. When they had dumped him into the bed they found her still in the hall. She waited until the barn man had gone, then told Murdock with cold anger, "They've been looking for you. Bluett is mad. I wouldn't be surprised if he fired you. I hope he does."

She tossed her head and ran down the stairs.

Chapter Twelve

Ken Murdock had little experience with hangovers. Building the ranch had left him neither time nor money to spend in saloons. He woke feeling that the top of his head was separated from the rest of him by a layer of blankness just above his ears. He moved, then squeezed his eyes shut and groaned. A whirling glimpse of daylight told him it was morning and habit forced him to get out of bed.

The rest of the boarders were already at the breakfast table when he came down. Stucki was there, showing no ill effect from his heavy night, delighting the others with a roaring account of the adventure with Buck Shaw.

Murdock kept his eyes on his plate, eating methodically, not because he wanted the food but in the hope that it would dull the threatening nausea.

Sheila was not in the room and he left as soon as possible,

grateful to escape facing her but dismally anticipating the confrontation with Bluett. His stomach sank further when Bluett told him in an expressionless voice that Sutro wanted to see him in the private boardroom.

Adolph Sutro was seldom at the tunnel office. Most of the time he was in San Francisco or the nation's and European capitals trying to drum up funds, but on this of all mornings he was at the long, paper-littered table, flanked by Sheldon and Doctor Brierly.

An ominous silence fell over them as Murdock gingerly stepped in. True, Sutro had the reputation of being a fair employer. Though the tunnel had never paid wages as high as some of the mines he had established a kind of employer care over his workmen unheard of in industry at the time. He was also known as a stern judge.

His voice rumbled heavily. "You didn't show up for work last night. Neither did your man Stucki."

Murdock advanced to the edge of the table. His knees felt weak and he was still not sure his breakfast would stay down. He said flatly, "We were drunk."

Sutro was surprised. He had heard all kinds of excuses, but this was a new one.

"So you were drunk. You expect the work to stop because you can't let the bottle alone?"

"No sir." Murdock glanced at Sheldon as if for help and found none there.

Sutro studied him, let him sweat awhile before he said, "I've heard no complaints about your drinking. Stucki, yes. He's come near being fired before. But you, how often have you been hitting the bottle?"

"Never before."

"Ah? Then you must have a special reason this time? You know drinking is not tolerated underground. You know how dangerous the work is, that every man must be alert at all times not only for his own sake but for the safety of the others."

"Yes, sir."

"And as head of the tunnel police you are a special case. On your shoulders rests a heavy responsibility."

"Yes, sir."

Murdock was getting tired of saying it. He had been a

little ashamed of himself when he came in. Now he was getting mad, thinking back on what Sutro had done to him and what he had done for Sutro.

"Well, boy, what is this exceptional reason?"

Ken Murdock talked fast. In telling about being jumped by Buck Shaw he took occasion to remind them that it was this same man who had tried to keep Sutro from going through the Savage, and made the point that he would probably be dead now if Stucki had not come to his rescue. When he paused for want of breath, Sutro said drily, "And you felt a celebration was called for?"

Murdock thought of Sutro defying Gillette, then celebrating at the French Rotisserie, and his next words slipped out unintentionally.

"Wouldn't you?"

A twinkle winked in the heavy-lidded eyes and the judicial tone changed to a probing interest.

"What were you doing in Virginia?"

Murdock drew himself up stiffly. "I was there on some personal business."

A silkiness slipped into Sutro's voice. "Virginia is, after all, a rather small city. Much personal business becomes a matter of general knowledge. You did go to the Powell brokerage office yesterday afternoon, did you not?"

Murdock was startled. "Well—yes."

"Are you by chance trading in stocks?"

Murdock's anger returned with a rush. "You know better than that. Your people sold my brother all the stock I'll ever want to buy."

"Then we can say you went to see Miss Powell?"

Murdock nearly choked. "Let's leave her name out of this."

Sutro appeared amused by something. "You know, Ken," the voice was more friendly, "you aren't the first man to be twisted around a woman's finger."

"I . . ."

"Everyone in town has been watching you. You see, Helen Powell had created quite a titillating reputation for herself."

"I said leave her out. It's my business and . . ."

"No." Sutro whipped at him. "It is my business, I think. I

believe that her only interest in you was the information you could give her about our underground operations."

"I . . ."

"She is not the first stock trader to try to plant a spy in our workings."

Murdock felt the breath knocked out of him. He did not know how to answer. He had not realized that he was not supposed to talk about Sutro or the tunnel. He stood blank-faced. A corner of Sutro's mouth lifted.

"Never mind. I could have warned you or fired you weeks ago. I did not, because I wanted you to do exactly what you did."

Sheldon lifted his head in his own surprise. Murdock had at least that comfort, and Sutro was continuing, explaining now, like a teacher.

"Stockbrokers have an unfortunate vanity. They think no one else understands the market. But I knew that sooner or later they would get interested in my stock. It was bound to happen and I have watched them closely, your friend Miss Powell among them."

Murdock was out of his depth and knew it. He held his tongue and listened carefully. There was so much in what had happened that he did not comprehend.

"I was delighted when she showed a marked interest in you. It made an opportunity for me to feed you what information I wanted her to have. If I had told her directly, she would have suspected trickery and not moved. I wanted her syndicate to start buying, to make a market for the stock. I could have done that myself, through my own brokers, but again it would have been suspect. It was necessary that outsiders do it, make the price rise so that the general public would smell value and invest."

Ken Murdock lifted a hand to interrupt him. "May I ask a question?"

"Good. As many as you want."

"When I told her you were issuing company stock she came apart, said she was ruined. Is that so?"

"Not ruined. At least not yet, not until settlement date."

"What's that mean?"

"Do you know what buying on margin means?"

"No."

The tunnel man smiled. "I will illustrate. Assume a stock has a market value of ten dollars a share and you place an order for one share on margin. You put up one dollar and your broker borrows from the bank the other nine dollars, against the share you are buying. Now, if the price of your stock goes up, you can sell it for more than ten dollars and have a profit. But if it goes down, you must either put up more money yourself or lose both the stock and the margin you have paid in. Do you see that?"

Murdock brightened. "Yes . . ."

"So. Here is what happened to Miss Powell and her friends. They created an unnatural market in tunnel stock by buying a great many shares. No one has been trading in it for months and their sudden activity brought it to people's attention. A lot of speculators who are always watching for a bargain thought the activity meant that someone knew something the general public did not know, and they stepped in and bought too, and that pushed the price up further.

"That was what we had been waiting for, that rise. That made it worth while for us to release a hundred thousand shares of treasury stock."

Murdock understood that, but another angle puzzled him. "Why did you let me hear that the company was selling the stock if you knew I'd tell Miss Powell?"

Sutro chuckled. "We sold all the stock before you could tell her. We needed that three hundred thousand to finish the ditch and the lateral tunnels, but I didn't want the Powell syndicate to get in any deeper. I didn't want them to go broke, only to stop buying."

Murdock's head was spinning although the hangover had been driven out of him. "But in effect you robbed them and the public of three hundred thousand dollars."

"No, boy, no. Let's call it a forced loan. All they have to do is hold the stock until the mine contracts are signed. Then it will go even higher than what they paid for it. I haven't robbed anyone of anything."

Ken Murdock bent across the table in a quick eagerness. "Would it be all right if I told her that?"

Sutro looked at him stolidly. He almost said, "Keep far away from that woman, she can only mean trouble for you."

94

He did not. Every man was entitled to his own mistakes. He lifted his thick shoulders.

"Tell her whatever you want."

Murdock hurried out, hurried to the boarding house. He found Stucki playing checkers with Jack Bryan and told him to cover his day shift, then ran upstairs for his gun. He did not intend to be caught unarmed in Virginia again.

He came out of the room, fastening the belt around his waist, and nearly ran over Sheila as she stepped from the doorway across the hall. Her eyes went to the heavy weapon, then up to his face in sympathy.

"You don't have to work this morning—after last night . . . ?"

He sounded defensive. "Going to Virginia."

"For Mr. Sutro?"

He had had enough of questions and it made him short. "For myself."

The girl's sympathy vanished and she turned waspish. "To get drunk again, I suppose?"

He knew he was being silly. He did not want to quarrel with her but somehow he could not stop.

"If I want to, yes."

"Go on. Go on. I'm sure it's of no interest to me."

She seemed always to be marching away from him in anger. He almost called after her, then did not, but dropped down the stairs quickly and left the house.

He used the rig in which he had brought Stucki home, to return it to the livery. All the way to Dayton and up the twisting mountain grade he rehearsed what he meant to say to Helen Powell, but when the rig was delivered and he was on the street an unwillingness to face the girl overcame him. He loitered along the sidewalk, stalling against reaching the office.

It was not as busy as it had been the day before and there was a silent pall that made him think of funerals. He asked a clerk for her and was told in a hushed voice that she was in her private office. He knocked, heard her weary answer and pushed the door open.

Her drawn face broke with surprise, then clouded. "I told you not to come here again. Don't you hear well?"

All the speeches he had made up deserted him. To cover

95

his confusion he took his time closing the door. When he turned to her again she had risen behind her table.

"Well?"

"I want just a few minutes—to talk to you."

"There is nothing to say."

"It won't cost you anything to listen. I was with Sutro this morning."

Her sharp rejection died on her lips. She was too good a gambler to pass up any possible advantage.

"And?"

He was blunt with the edge of rising anger. "He told me you've been using me. He's not the only one who's said it but I didn't believe it before."

She lifted her chin, not answering.

"He also said he'd known it and deliberately fed me information to get it to you."

Her mouth pressed tight, bringing a white ring around her red lips.

"So Adolph used us." She said it to herself, not to him.

He found a stiff smile. "I'm a greenhorn at this game but Sutro says he didn't want you ruined and that you won't be if you hang on until the stalemate with the mines is broken."

In her first panic of the day before she had ordered sold every share that showed a profit at the falling levels, but common sense had come to her rescue and she had stopped selling before they began to show a loss. She weighed the possibilities now, trying to judge how long they could hold on, how long her credit and that of the syndicate members could meet the margin requirements. She sat down slowly.

Her laugh was brittle. "And how long will that be?"

"We're driving the laterals now. Every foot that they advance, every foot of ditch that's finished is building pressure on the mines. And they're still talking with Sutro. They'd stop the talks if they dared."

"How can I trust what Sutro says? I can't even trust you now."

For the first time he saw the cold calculation in her eyes, saw the shrewd self-concern that was the only basis for her interest in him. With that he admitted that he had indeed made a complete fool of himself. And suddenly he was free,

96

in control, and his own man again. His words came even, easily.

"I don't really care whether you believe me or not, but I wanted to tell you that I did not consciously try to lead you to ruin yourself. Goodbye."

He reached for the door but she stopped him. "Will you do one more thing for me?"

Over his shoulder he said, "What?"

"Let me know when the first mine signs the contract. Before the news is general?"

"No."

She bit her lip, scrabbling for something to say, some method of bringing him back into line. Murdock did not give her the time. He opened the door, went through and closed it.

Helen Powell drummed thoughtfully on the table with her nails. Then she called a clerk and sent him to summon the syndicate members. They gathered within an hour, and the meeting was long and angry. But at its end they had all agreed to throw whatever they could of credit into the pot to meet the coming margin requirements as they rose.

Chapter Thirteen

The Powell meeting was not the only one held in Virginia that afternoon. Adolph Sutro had followed Murdock up the mountain for yet another conference in his rooms at the International Hotel with the representatives of the mineowners.

Behind these men were many millions of dollars. The companies for which they appeared had produced a wealth that had created a state out of the barren mountains and deserts of Nevada. It had founded fortunes that would continue down through the years. It had changed San Francisco from a struggling frontier town into a city that ranked with the glittering capitals of the world.

No one questioned the power of the companies. They had elected senators, governors, representatives. They dominated the money markets of the West. And as long as the silver continued to flow out of the mountain the power would go unchecked.

Sutro had fought them almost singlehanded. They had not stopped him. And now with that sixth sense cherished by all true gamblers he sensed that he was near his final victory.

He had made a discovery that the men facing him believed was their tightest guarded secret. A new disaster threatened the mines and, if it were known, their stocks would go into another dizzy drop.

Deep within the Savage, the Hale and Norcross, the Gould and Curry, great rivers of underground water had been tapped. The mines had always been wet. The seepage from the rock faces had been superheated, dangerous, but until now the big pumps had been able to control it.

They could not handle the new floods. The water level in the sumps was rising. It was only a matter of time until it spilled over and stopped all work in the lower drifts.

Sutro's spies had reported on the losing battle to contain that water for days. He faced his adversaries doubly confident. Besides that secret, the sale of the treasury stock had brought the money needed to complete the laterals and the ditch. Together he felt they gave him the whip hand.

He directed his attention to Gillette. The Savage superintendent was the key. While all of the mines were interconnected it was only the Savage that had a direct opening into the tunnel.

"We have been at odds for a long time, gentlemen," he said. "But the time for fighting is past, and I think you realize it."

They sat impassive, long schooled in the cat-and-mouse game. Gillette spoke for all.

"I can't see where the situation is changed. The charges you're asking are out of proportion. We can't and won't pay them."

"There is a change," Sutro said. "Now you've got to have my drainage ditch to take off your new flooding."

It was good to watch them stiffen, look at each other,

wonder how he had got the information. Gillette tried to pass it off with a light shrug.

"If you'd cut your charges fifty per cent we might do some business."

Sutro reddened, all the indignities he had suffered at the hands of these men, all the slights crowding upon him, roughening his voice.

"Those rates were established in an original agreement that was signed six years ago. They're not going to be shaved one nickel. You'll pay them because you have to."

The Hale and Norcross man whispered against Gillette's ear and Gillette smiled.

"Adolph, you always did underestimate the other fellow. You are not in the driver's seat. Certainly we have water, always have had. We've licked it before and we'll lick it this time—or simply pump it into your damn tunnel. Then where the hell do you think you'll be?"

Sutro stretched out a forefinger, shaking it. "Gillette, I warned you once—not to blow that hole in your drift. You wouldn't listen and a lot of men nearly died because of it. I'll warn you again. You dump water on us and you're in real trouble."

There was a general smiling around the group. Gillette laughed. "What do you think you can do about it?"

"We can close our bulkhead and force the stuff back on you."

Gillette spread his hands, raised his brows, looked at the others. He might as well have said *Crazy Adolph* aloud.

"Come on, Adolph, you can't build a bulkhead that will stop that kind of pressure. Ask any engineer."

"This one will." Sutro spaced the words out. "Just try it and see." He stood up and walked around the table. "Make yourselves at home as long as you like, gentlemen. When you get ready to sign you can reach me at the tunnel office." He went out, closing the door, leaving the strained silence behind.

One man grunted. "He's bluffing, just like he's tried to do before."

"I'm not too sure." It was Gillette. "Something in the way he said that worries me. If we did pump our sumps into the tunnel and the bulkhead did hold he'd have us by the short hairs for sure."

A musing voice down the table said, "I've heard a lot of rumors about that bulkhead, but who's seen it? Could it be a cute bit of imagination nicely leaked?"

There was a silence while they chewed over that idea, then Hale and Norcross said, "We'd better get a man down there to find out."

"They've got guards in the station under the Savage. One of them keeps making an ass of Buck Shaw. And nobody can get by Bluett's office."

"There has to be some way. Can't Shaw buy one of the guards?"

Gillette nodded absently, his mind still on his first reaction.

"It's worth a try, but if we find there is a bulkhead and it's strong enough to back the water up—what then?"

"We can always sign with Adolph."

"Not on his terms. No. I'll get Shaw on it."

Gillette led the group out of the hotel, went to his own office and sent for Buck Shaw. When the head of the mine police came in, Gillette said without looking up, "I've got a delicate job for you."

Shaw stood like a soldier at attention. He knew Gillette's ruthlessness and both respected and feared him.

"I want you to get a man into the tunnel. Sutro claims they have a bulkhead that will keep us from pumping our water down there. We want to know if he has it or is bluffing."

"It won't be easy. They've got that breakthrough covered day and night."

Gillette's voice was sour. "If I thought it was easy I wouldn't bother you with it. Give a guard a couple of hundred dollars to let us in for five minutes."

Shaw's mouth twisted with bitterness. "The head of their police is a tough nut."

Gillette raised his head then. "So get to one of his crew. He can't stay in that damned hole twenty-four hours a day."

Shaw went out smiling tightly to himself. Here was a way by which he could get back at Murdock, even if not directly. There was a clerk in Sheldon's office who was also on Gillette's payroll, a man named Hawkins who ought to know which of Murdock's guards would be vulnerable.

The immediate problem was to contact Hawkins. Neither

Shaw nor his men could walk into the tunnel office, and he did not know Hawkins' habits off duty. Then he thought of his new recruit, a drifter who had hit him for a job only a few days before and who was not yet known to be connected with the mine police.

Shaw located him without trouble and sent him down the hill. His cover was to ask Bluett for a job in the tunnel. His mission to pass a note to Hawkins. With that accomplished, Shaw had several hours to kill, waiting for the result of his first move.

At six in the evening he was in a small, unsavory bar in the gully below C Street. At six-thirty Hawkins walked in and joined him, a wizened, uncertain, pale creature whose only love in life was the figures in his ledgers. He accepted Shaw's whiskey with an obsequious dip of his birdlike head, listened to what Shaw wanted and pouted his blue lips. He had heard rumors about the bulkhead but had paid no attention to anything that went on back in the dark reaches.

"I just want to get to one of the police," Shaw told him. "Can't you set that up?"

The pout became painful. "Murdock—he wouldn't talk to his mother."

"I know that." Buck Shaw had trouble always with keeping his patience. "But there are others. One named Stucki." He poured another drink.

The clerk drank before he shook his head. "He likes money but he likes Murdock better. Murdock licked him."

Shaw arched one eyebrow. "He should want to even it up."

Hawkins' words were precise, prissy. "I would have expected that because he was quite a bully—called himself Chief until Murdock whipped him. It's odd, but now he trails Murdock around like a puppy dog. I just don't know who . . ."

Buck Shaw filled the glasses again. "There has to be someone we can reach. The boss is willing to spend dough, maybe five hundred." He was stretching Gillette's figure but he knew he was safe, if he brought it off. A few hundred one way or the other was not important to a man running a silver mine that produced up to a million dollars' worth of the blue ore a month.

Hawkins licked his lips. It gave Shaw another idea.

"There's an added hundred for you if you get me the right boy."

The little clerk worried over the problem until Shaw thought he would cry. Then a craftiness glinted in the weak eyes.

"I wonder—there is one—he was Murdock's friend, then the girl he wants to marry lost her head over Murdock and there is a rift. Al Temple—he might ..."

"What shift does he work?"

"The four to midnight. We seldom see each other ..."

Shaw spilled coins on the table and shoved them at Hawkins. "Make a point of it. You get the other fifty if Temple meets me here by three o'clock tomorrow morning."

He watched the clerk claw the coins into a purse and scurry out. He went to an obscure restaurant for supper and then, with some hours to get through, he sought one of the dark houses in the hollow to take his mind off the dragging time.

Al Temple came off his shift into the clear night and dawdled behind his team as they headed for the boarding house. The biting air was refreshing after the fumes that continued to generate in the tunnel. He was a block behind them when a black shadow scuttled out from against a house wall to intercept him. He dropped his hand to his gun, then let it fall as he recognized the little clerk from the office, a man he had small use for.

"Temple," There was whiskey on Hawkins' breath as he lifted to his toes to put his mouth close to Temple's face. "Al, I know a way for you to make some quick money—easily."

Temple backed away in distaste. He almost brushed the clerk off, but it was an odd coincidence. He had spent the boring hours of the shift this night as he had for weeks mulling over the possibilities of doing just what Hawkins suggested. He knew that Sheila Bryan was in love with Murdock, but Murdock was infatuated with the Powell woman. If he had money enough to get married he felt sure he could make her give up on Murdock and accept him. But the tunnel job, even with the bonus Murdock had got for him, was not enough to sway her. What he needed was a stake. He stood where he was.

"How much?"

Hawkins' whisper told how impressed he was with the figure. "Five hundred dollars."

Al Temple's mouth twisted. "Do you know what they'd do if they caught me robbing the Con Virginia strong box?"

"Oh dear, it's nothing like that." Hawkins was shocked. "Someone in Virginia just wants to peek at our bulkhead, just to see that it exists. That's all."

Al Temple was silent, his lips tightening, looking down on the shrunken figure. Hawkins began to be frightened. If Temple told Bluett or Sheldon about this conversation he would lose his job. He hurried on.

"It can't hurt to let just one man in to see it. You can stand by and make sure he doesn't do anything to it. All they want is to learn if Sutro is bluffing. Just meet Buck Shaw at the Red Bull saloon before three o'clock this morning. He'll tell you the same thing. There's no harm in it."

Al Temple stepped past the clerk and left him groaning in fear. He walked through the night feeling the breeze chill the sweat that started on his forehead. He argued with himself. What harm was there? The mineowners were being bullheaded. They ought to sign with Sutro, should have long ago. They had threatened to dump their water on the tunnel before it was ready. Might this not be a way to prove to them what would happen in their mines if they did?

He stopped abruptly. He was not at the door of the boarding house. Unconsciously his feet had answered his dilemma. He was at the livery barn.

He came into the Red Bull at two-thirty, and spotted Buck Shaw at a rear table, watching the door. Shaw rose quietly and strolled through the door of the back room, leaving the panel ajar.

Temple looked over the rest of the main room. It was filled but he saw no one he knew. He moved back carelessly as if he had no real purpose, stopped for a little beside a poker table and stood watching the play. Then he wandered on and into the back room.

Shaw was at the table there, facing the door, a bottle and

two glasses before him. He nodded to the chair across from him.

"Sit down, Temple, join me in a drink while we talk."

He kept his tone casual, almost friendly. He would have liked to sneer, to mock a man who would set his price at a handful of silver coins, rub his nose in his cheapness. But this was a touchy interview. Temple might be the only one he could buy. He did not want him backing off, having second thoughts. There was also the chance that the tunnel guard was not here to sell himself but to learn from Shaw how much Gillette considered the look at the bulkhead was worth, to report back to Sutro. He had been very careful with his liquor tonight, to keep a clear head.

Covertly he watched Temple's hesitant steps. That was a good sign, that and the way the blond man eased down into the chair as if ready to spring up and run if he suspected trickery. After his first glance Shaw kept his eyes lowered, did not look directly at the other. He poured the glasses, shoved one across, then took a leather pouch from his pocket, opened the string and shook out a cascade of glittering gold pieces.

Talk, promises were one thing. Some men did not believe promises. But the sight of gold did something to any man. He arranged them in five neat piles, five coins to each pile. Twenty-dollar gold pieces. One at a time he moved the piles across the table as if he were moving checkers across a board. Temple did not move. He did not touch the coins. He did not touch the glass.

Shaw made his voice as soft as he could. "We'd like one of our engineers to have a five-minute look at your bulkhead. Just five minutes. A hundred dollars a minute for you."

Al Temple tried to speak, choked on his dry throat and tried again.

"I can't do it."

Buck Shaw's eyes came up then, hooded. "Why not? You stand guard at the breakthrough, four to midnight, don't you?"

"Yes."

"So all you have to do is let our engineer down, then boost him back up."

"I'm not alone there. There are always two of us."

"Can't you send him on an errand? Say about seven-thirty tomorrow night?"

Temple's eyes were glued to the gold piles. "They're working on the lateral tunnels . . ."

"In sight of the bulkhead?"

"Well—no."

"Five hundred dollars, Temple . . ."

Al Temple choked again on what he had come here to say. "Five hundred isn't enough. Maybe I could take the chance for a thousand."

Shaw's mouth tightened to shut off his grin. "Why a thousand?"

"I need that much to go away."

"You mean the girl won't go with you unless you have that much?"

Temple started. How could Shaw know about Sheila? But he could not think about that now. He needed his wits to make his bargain.

"I need it to move, to live on until I get a job."

"All right. A thousand it is." Even at that price Shaw knew Gillette would not argue. "Take the five hundred now. The engineer will have the rest tomorrow night."

Temple reached for a deep breath and pressed his gamble. "No. All of it now." He did not want to spend the intervening hours worrying whether Shaw would renege and leave him in a spot where he was vulnerable yet without enough to take Sheila away.

This time Shaw hesitated for so long that Temple wanted to shout. Finally he leaned back and dug into another pocket and one by one dropped another twenty-five coins among the others. Then contemptuously he tossed the pouch on top of them.

"Put it in that so you don't mislay any of it."

Temple fumbled the coins into the purse. "What—what if I take it and can't live up to the bargain?"

"You'll live up to it," Shaw said pleasantly. "You'd better if you want to be around to enjoy that girl."

Chapter Fourteen

Al Temple felt very good as he turned the horse over to the hostler and walked through the bright morning to the boarding house.

In the dining room the early shift was at breakfast. The graveyard crew would not come from the tunnel for another hour. He found an empty chair and dropped into it, smiling at his neighbors, nodding coolly to Murdock. When these men left for work the house would be empty for a little while. It would give him a chance to talk to Sheila without too much fear of interruption.

The maids served him and the crew was gone by the time he finished. He felt tension rise in him as he went to the kitchen.

The girl was not there. Jack Bryan was, unshaven, his hair still rumpled from his night asleep, having a cup of coffee to dispell his morning grouch. Temple knew better than to speak to him. He went past the table to one of the girls, asking in a low voice where Sheila was.

"Upstairs making beds, I guess."

He touched her shoulder in thanks and took the rear stairs. Sheila was in his and Murdock's room, but not making beds. She was sitting on the edge of Murdock's mattress, her hands over her face. She looked up, startled by him, and with a shock he saw that she was crying.

He hauled up in the doorway for a helpless second, then hurried forward, caught her arms and crouched before her.

"Sheila—what is it?"

"It's nothing—nothing. Let me alone for a minute. I'll be all right."

"But ..."

"Please. Don't talk to me right now. Just give me a minute."

He stood up, staring down at her, then turned to his own

106

bunk, fussing with the covers, trying to show that he respected her privacy, trying to help.

"You can turn around now."

When he did, she had wiped at her eyes with a handkerchief and held it balled in her fist. Her eyes were swollen but her voice was nearly normal. He came to stand close to her.

"Don't you want to tell me about it?"

Her lip curled ruefully. "It's silly. I got to feeling sorry for myself and suddenly I was crying—for no reason at all."

"Murdock?"

She started to shake her head, then nodded instead. "I just hate to see him be so stupid. I thought he was going to quit last night. I think he still may. I guess he had a fight with her."

Temple did not have to ask who *her* was. Silently he cursed Ken Murdock, but at the same time he thought that the man who had been his friend had possibly done him a favor.

"Sheila, he's a simpleton—a hick cowboy who lost his ranch and got his head turned by a woman who knows more about life than he'll ever guess. He's not worth your tears."

She did not answer and that gave him courage.

"I love you," he said. "You know that. Enough even that if I thought it would do any good I'd try to beat some sense into his hard head. But it wouldn't. And I couldn't lick him anyway."

A trace of a smile tugged at her lips for a moment. On impulse she reached for his hand.

"I'm sorry, Al. I like you, but . . ."

"But Murdock. Are you going to throw away your life pining over him? Sheila, this is no place for you. No place for me either. I'll never make anything in the tunnel or the mines either. In San Francisco I could, I know it. Marry me and we'll go there. I'll show you."

Her hand tightened on his. "Thanks, Al, but it wouldn't work. It wouldn't be fair to you, feeling the way I do."

He put his other hand over hers, holding it captive, and put everything he had into his argument, knowing that if he were ever to be able to convince her it had to be now.

"Many women have married men they didn't love at first,

and had happy marriages. You like me. We like the same things. We'll make it work. Just give me the chance."

"It takes money to get married, to travel, to set up a place to live."

Elation exploded like a light in him. He was sure that he had won her. Hurriedly he pulled the pouch out and spilled the heavy coins on the bed.

"I've got money. Plenty to keep us until I get a new start."

She looked down at the bright pile. It was more money than she had ever seen at one time. Slowly she lifted her eyes to his face.

"Where did you get that?"

He stammered, caught off guard. He had not got as far as thinking up a story about the gold and his voice roughened with his embarrassment.

"There are a lot of ways for a man to make money."

"You've been gambling."

Relief flooded through him. He wondered why it had not occurred to him. Everybody on the Comstock gambled, day and night. In stocks, with dice, with cards.

"That's right. I got lucky."

She bent to put out one finger, turn one coin over. But her voice was dull.

"I could never marry a gambler."

Panic reached for him, gave his words a breathless sound. "I'm not a gambler. Honest. I just got lucky, that's all. I—I got to thinking about you and how I didn't have anything to offer you and, well, I decided to take a chance—and I won."

"At poker?"

He had sense enough to steer away from that. If he said poker, she might ask who was in the game, who lost.

"At roulette. At the Crystal. The wheel was running hot. On red. I played red. I kept doubling. You made my luck."

She did not think to doubt his story. There had been too many reports of fabulous wins. One of the biggest mineowners on the Lode had got his start by winning ten thousand dollars in a single night. But she sighed.

"And now you've got the bug. You won't be content until you try to win a lot more."

"I promise you."

108

"I know. You forget that I've been raised with men. I know them and their weaknesses. That money will burn a hole in your pocket and you'll get to thinking that you did this once and that you can do it again—and again."

He moved suddenly, scooped the coins back into the pouch and wrapped her hands around it.

"You keep it, then I won't be tempted."

She held it toward him. "Al—I can't do that."

He backed away. "Why not? It's for us. If you won't marry me it's no good to me. Keep it. Think about it. Please."

Then, before she could come near him and force it back upon him, he turned and strode out of the room.

Chapter Fifteen

Al Temple was not a devious person and he had always considered himself fairly honest. His rationale was genuine enough—that if the mineowners convinced themselves that Sutro's bulkhead would really hold back their water, they would have to give in. And he meant to make sure that the engineer could not do anything to damage it.

He was at peace with his conscience when the time came for him to relieve Murdock at the breakthrough.

He walked through the tunnel rather than riding an ore car. He stopped to investigate the first blower, then went on. At the second he cut off the valve. With any luck the fact that it was not working would not be noticed until he wanted it to be. With the ventilation system helped by the connection with the Savage, the tunnel did not get as hot as it had before.

The job of guarding the connecting hole was boring. There was nothing to do except sit and make sure no one came down from the mine. Tonight Pierce was sharing the watch with Temple, the rest of the shift crew strung out at intervals. Pierce was older, perhaps forty, an ex-teamster. Bluett had hired him after a winter storm had caught him and frostbitten his face so badly that he could no longer work outside.

He amused himself by sitting on a rock in the station and whittling figures from pieces of Ponderosa pine. Temple watched him with deliberate interest, rising from time to time to stand beneath the hole and listen for sounds from above, using those routine moves to sneak glances at his watch. Five minutes before seven-thirty he ran a finger around his throat inside his collar.

"Hot in here."

The man became aware, looked around, nodded.

"I don't think the blower's working." Temple walked to the air pipes, tested them and shook his head. "It isn't. We'll smother before the end of the shift if it isn't fixed. Hike back to the vent shaft and see."

Pierce frowned at the idea of the long walk.

Temple said, "I'd go, I'd rather be moving than sitting here doing nothing, but you know the orders. A foreman has to be here at all times. I can't leave until Stucki shows up and that'll be better than four hours."

Pierce closed his knife deliberately and dropped it into his pocket. He took his time. It seemed to Temple that he would never get to his feet, never move down the tunnel and out of sight of the bulkhead. But finally he was gone.

Temple stood tense, waiting. He could hear the crews working at the faces of the laterals. If one of them happened to come back into the main tunnel in the next few minutes, there would be hell to pay. But it was a chance he had to take. He was sweating by the time he heard the grate of boots on the floor of the Savage drift overhead.

A hollow voice came down. "Temple?"

"Yeah."

"I'm Bob Norse. Shaw said you'd expect me. How is it down there?"

"All right, but make it fast."

A coil of rope dropped at Temple's feet, one end running up through the hole. The engineer slid down it quickly.

"Now where's this famous bulkhead?"

Temple turned down the tunnel without answer, stepped through the thick doorway and stood watching down the dark corridor. From the corner of his eye he could see Norse critically examine the rock walls from which the masonry of the bulkhead jutted, see him assess the design by which, with the doors closed, water pressure behind would force the whole structure tighter together and against the narrowing walls. Then Norse gave a low whistle and turned back toward the breakthrough. Temple walked behind him, backward, watching for movement down the tunnel.

Norse said quietly, "Whoever designed that knew what he was doing."

Temple barely turned his head. "Sutro did."

Norse grunted. "The more I learn about Adolph the more impressed I get. How's our timing?"

"Close."

"I'll be gone in a minute. Just stand on that rope to keep it taut."

Temple felt a hand pressed against his shoulder blades to stop him and saw that they were back at the hole. He planted both feet on the coil, pulling the rope in front of him so that he could still watch. Norse went up like a seasoned sailor and a moment later the rope was tugged on, pulled up as Temple released it.

Temple went to lean against the wall, conscious of the heat, conscious of the weakness in his legs. He was still there when Pierce came back, growling that some idiot had turned the blower off.

It took Temple the rest of the shift to relax, to be convinced that no one had seen him and Norse and reported to Bluett. It was not until he was out of the tunnel, walking unchallenged to the boarding house that he believed he had turned the trick and was free.

And he was certain that he had done nothing to impair Sutro's fight.

111

Chapter Sixteen

At ten o'clock on the following Saturday morning, Gillette of the Savage, flanked by the engineer Norse and two attornies, walked into the Storey County courthouse and asked for and received a temporary injunction from Judge Rising against the tunnel company and Adolph Sutro or any of his representatives.

The writ was a restraining order on all work on the tunnel until after the hearing, and Sutro was directed to appear in court the following week to show cause why the injunction should not be made permanent.

It was further stipulated that until the hearing was over, Sutro and his employees were enjoined from closing the bulkhead.

None of the tunnel officers knew anything about the action. Sutro had gone to San Francisco on the morning train and Sheldon was in charge.

The first tunnel men to hear about the writ were Ken Murdock and Bishop, foreman of the men working in the laterals. They were discussing the work at the faces when the guard at the breakthrough station called to the bulkhead.

"Hey, Ken. There's a guy trying to come down from the mine. He says he's the sheriff."

Murdock ran, with Bishop at his heels. When they reached the station they found that a burly man in miner's clothes had already dropped down a rope ladder. There were other men in the Savage drift but they were not trying to enter the tunnel.

The burly man was saying, "Who's in charge of the work here?"

Bishop was in nominal charge of the crew. He said, "I guess I am."

"I am Sheriff Williamson." The man pulled a paper from

112

his pocket. "This is a temporary injunction to stop all work in the tunnel until the hearing next week."

Bishop looked at Murdock helplessly. "What's that mean?"

The sheriff's voice was short. "Exactly what it says. Anybody who does a lick of work down here from this minute on is liable to arrest for contempt of court."

"I don't know about such things." Bishop scratched his head. "I've got no authority to stop the work. You'd better see Mr. Sheldon."

"Where is he?"

"At the tunnel office, I guess."

"Then give him the writ." The sheriff shoved it into Bishop's hand and climbed back up the ladder.

Bishop unfolded the paper with its imposing seal. "Ken, what's this all about? Can a judge tell a bunch of men they can't work?"

Murdock did not know.

Bishop held the paper forward gingerly. "If I go out to the office with this, Sheldon will eat my tail off for leaving the job. How about you taking it? I'll put one of my crew on guard until you get back."

Murdock debated. He was not supposed to leave this post. He could send his other guard. The writ looked important and Murdock had a fearful respect for the power of the courts. Had not a judge in Oregon ordered the foreclosure of his ranch? But it might be that Sheldon would need him in a hurry for some counteracting move. He took the paper and made the long trip to the office.

Bluett and Sheldon were together when he came into the room. Both looked at him in surprise. Bluett said, "What are you doing here? Who's at the breakthrough?"

"One of Bishop's crew and Baily."

Bluett's face reddened. "You or Temple or Stucki are expected to be there at all times."

For answer Murdock laid the paper on the desk. Bluett frowned at it, picked it up and unfolded it.

"Where'd this come from?"

"A man who said he was Sheriff Williamson came down through the Savage and gave it to Bishop."

"Why'd you let him down?"

113

"I was at the bulkhead. He came before I could stop him."

"You had orders to shoot anybody who tried . . ."

Murdock said into the pause, "A sheriff?"

Bluett was out of words for the moment. Sheldon reached for the paper.

"What is it?"

Bluett passed it to him and as Sheldon read, exploded.

"I don't believe it. Why should Judge Rising order a work stop? Why an order not to close the bulkhead? Do you suppose the Savage bastards are getting ready to dump their stinking water on us?"

Sheldon's throat was constricted. "It seems to be in order . . ."

Bluett was raging. "It's another of Gillette's tricks. Trying to put the screws on Sutro."

Sheldon was already on his way to the telegraph room. He came back too quickly, cursing.

"The damned thing never works when we need it. I'll have to go to Virginia and find out what this is all about."

Through his spluttering, Bluett said, "You'd better take Murdock with you. You don't know what they might try."

"No," Sheldon said. "I want Murdock back at the breakthrough. Tell Bishop to go ahead with the work until I learn if this is valid. Ken, unless that telegraph is fixed it will take me about four hours to make the round trip. Can you handle the duty that long? I don't want to depend on Stucki or Temple either."

"I can," Murdock said, and hurried back through the tunnel.

He found the lateral crews grouped around Bishop uncertainly and told them to go back to the job.

Bishop looked worried. "The man said we'd be in contempt of court . . ."

"And Bluett says it's a fake, a trick of Gillette's. Sheldon's gone to Virginia to talk to the lawyers and see the judge. He says to go ahead until he makes sure."

"Well—I only work here—" Bishop said, and sent his crews back to the lateral faces.

Sheldon pushed his horse up the grade but it was three in the afternoon before he reached the mining town. The courthouse was closed and he had difficulty locating the tunnel

114

lawyers. He found one playing whist at the Washoe club and together they went in search of Judge Rising.

They located him in a private poker game at the International Hotel and he objected to leaving until he had finished, winning a good pot. Then, grumbling, he went down to the bar with them, to a corner table.

Sheldon dropped the writ in front of him. "Is this authentic?"

The judge was a testy man. He flipped the paper open, glanced through it, his jaws tightening, and bobbed his head. "Of course it is. Thoroughly legal."

Sheldon was having trouble controlling his anger. "On what grounds did you issue it? What reason has the court to stop us? The tunnel was authorized by Congress. Our right of way was okayed by a Presidential commission, concurred to by the state of Nevada and the counties affected."

"This is only a temporary restraining order. You'll have your day in court next week. I don't think you understand the law very well, Mr. Sheldon."

"Who does?"

The judge glared at him. "Anyone can ask for a temporary injunction against nearly anything, the granting of it is practically automatic. It is the hearing that is important, when it is decided whether the injunction should be made permanent."

"A hell of a thing. You mean I could enjoin the Savage from working their sixteen-hundred-foot level?"

"If you could show cause that their work might constitute a danger to the property or to the men, yes."

"And just what did they show that makes our work a danger to them?"

"You have a bulkhead, I believe."

"What about it?"

The judge said angrily, "A mine engineer descended and examined it. He swore that the bulkhead constitutes a threat to the mine, that if it were closed and your laterals should tap flood water, it would back up into their lower drifts and endanger men and property."

Sheldon sat very still. Either the engineer was lying or one of his own guards had performed a treachery. He spread his fingers flat on the table.

"Your Honor, that is utter nonsense. The only water that

115

could back up from our workings would be their own sump water, pumped down on us. They have threatened to do that. It is one of the trump cards they're using in their game to avoid signing our contracts."

"Completely irrelevant, Mr. Sheldon."

Sheldon's voice rose in frustration. "It appears that everything is irrelevent that doesn't benefit the mine."

Rising's face flushed scarlet. "Sir, that is very close to being contempt of court."

Sheldon shoved back his chair. "This doesn't look like a court to me. It looks like a bar."

Trembling with his anger, he turned on his heel and stalked out. His lawyer caught him in the lobby.

"Take it easy, don't antagonize him. It won't buy us a thing. He can make the injunction stick if he chooses, and if he does make it permanent, we'll be in a hell of a fix."

Sheldon looked at him bitterly, brushed by him and went to the telegraph office. At least the wires were open to San Francisco. The message he sent to Sutro was a cry for help. Sheldon was in over his head and he knew it. He needed the steady hand of the old man.

Even as he sent the wire there was action deep beneath the very office in which he stood that would shake the city of Virginia to its honeycombed foundations.

Bishop's crews finished punching the drill holes on which they had been working when Sheriff Williamson interrupted them. They set their shots and fired them. The blasts were heard plainly in the Savage and word of them was relayed to Gillette in his office above. He sent for the sheriff but the officer could not immediately be found, so his deputy hurried to the mine.

Backed up by Buck Shaw and three mine police he stepped into the lift and was dropped to the sixteen-hundred-foot level, led along it to the breakthrough. As they went they could hear the rattle as broken rock was mucked into the waiting tunnel cars.

Hanging tight to the rope ladder, he was dropped again, so fast that he was on the floor before Ken Murdock could react.

Murdock, leaning against the wall close to the stoop that

116

had been cut out as a tool shed, straightened, slapping at his gun.

"Hey. You can't come down here."

"I am a deputy sheriff. You people are in contempt of court for ignoring the writ. You are all under arrest."

The pompous words shouted at the top of his voice carried to the men in the laterals. They dropped their tools and ran toward the station, but before they arrived Buck Shaw had plummeted to the deputy's side.

He stood loose, ready, hungry, his hand on his gun butt, his thin mouth twisted into a mocking grin.

"Well now, Murdock. This time you're on the wrong side of the law."

Murdock was acutely aware of that, looking at the badge glittering on the deputy's vest. He wished that he were a thousand miles away, but he could only remember Sheldon's warning. *Don't let anyone near that bulkhead.* He stood his ground.

"Shaw, you're no part of the sheriff's office. Climb back up where you belong."

Buck Shaw laughed at him. The deputy, watching the huge-shouldered men tumbling from the laterals, was not so confident. He was more than glad to let Shaw take over the play. Shaw did.

"Don't try it, Murdock, or if you do, do it now. I'd be pleasured to shoot your head off."

Murdock did not move a muscle. He said, "We've got eighteen men here. You might get me, but they'd club you to pulp. Just go, peaceful, while there's the chance."

Shaw only grinned, eager to goad Murdock into drawing. He had lusted to kill this man since their first meeting. He bawled at Bishop.

"Keep off. Unless you want a slug in your chest."

The foreman stopped, spreading his arms to block the men pouring in behind him. They were all unarmed. Only Murdock and his guard had guns and Baily made no sign that he would take a part of this.

Ken Murdock knew that he stood alone. He said tonelessly, "I will not tell either of you again. You're on tunnel property. You've got just two minutes to go up through that hole."

The deputy was watching his face. He had seen other men cornered before, forced to fight. The imposition of a writ was not a killing matter to him. Let the sheriff take care of it later, they had made their point. He shrugged and reached a hand toward the ladder.

Shaw used the movement as a diversion, thinking it would distract Murdock for the instant, and snapped his gun up.

It was a mistake. Murdock had not for a split second taken his attention off the mine policeman. He saw the tensing of Shaw's muscles, saw the twist of the wrist that brought the heavy gun out of the holster.

Shaw fired too quickly. His bullet grazed Murdock's cap, its breeze making the flame jump. He did not fire again. Murdock's action had mirrored his. The slug drove against Shaw's chest, knocked him backward and down.

The deputy was gaping. The action made him instinctively slap at his hip. Before he could draw, Murdock's second bullet broke his shoulder.

There was silence in the tunnel, heavy silence except for the ringing in their ears. The deputy had kept his feet but staggered against the wall. Then Bishop yelled from the mouth of the lateral.

"You killed him."

It was high-pitched, excited. Murdock could not tell whether it was pleased. Everyone hated the mine police. For himself he felt nothing but a certain numbness. His hand had reacted without a conscious order from his brain.

And then he heard the echo of Sheila's warning about a gun. *If you wear one you'll kill someone sooner or later.*

He turned his back on the fallen figure, crossed the station and leaned against the wall. It was very hot. The thick smell of burnt powder in the air made it hard to breathe. In a detached way he saw Bishop and his crew come forward. They helped the deputy climb the rope ladder, then they lifted Shaw's body and passed it up to the reaching hands of the mine police above. He saw Bishop come toward him. The foreman sounded very worried.

"You'd better get out of here fast. Gillette's got a lot of power. He won't rest until you hang."

Murdock filled his lungs. "Shaw drew first. You saw him."

He lowered himself onto his haunches where he was. He would not leave this place until Sheldon or Bluett told him to.

Chapter Seventeen

Sheriff Williamson had been visiting the Governor's office in Carson City. He returned to Virginia shortly after the wounded deputy had been brought up through the Savage and he listened to the report of the other mine police who had been in the drift in growing outrage.

Then he rounded up and deputized a group of twenty men and made the dizzying drop in the lift. They were all heavily armed but the narrowness of the passage and of the hole limited the number that could effectively be thrown into a fight.

There was no fight. The threat of the law had dampened the normal belligerence of the underground workmen and at Williamson's first hail they surrendered.

Murdock had no choice. He did not know whether he would have tried to stop the sheriff. Bishop standing close behind him when the challenge came, grabbed Murdock's gun from its holster and flipped it back over his head.

Murdock swung around on him but Bishop was shaking his head, saying, "We can't fight them. We'd just get some of the boys killed and it wouldn't do any good."

Murdock shot a glance toward the guard who had replaced Baily, a man named Tunney. Tunney's gun was in its holster and he had turned his back. As Murdock looked, the man took off, running down the tunnel.

Then Williamson had come down, his men behind him, backing the crew against the station wall, demanding, "Which one is Murdock?"

"I am." Ken stepped forward.

"Where's your gun?"

Ken's voice was toneless. "It was taken from me."

The sheriff did not believe him, ordered him searched, then

ordered the crew searched. No gun was found. Bishop's pitch had landed Ken's weapon at the back of the recessed tool stoop. Williamson was puzzled, but put that aside, raised his voice.

"All of you are under arrest, in contempt of court. Murdock, you are charged with murder."

Murdock gasped. "If you mean Buck Shaw, he drew first. He was trying to pick a fight. He's been after me ever since I came to Washoe."

The hard faces, the cold eyes of the posse were like a physical blow, and for the first time Ken was deeply afraid. He had faced death by gunfire, but this was different, a promise of inexorable pressure that he did not know how to combat. It made him sound breathless.

"I had orders to keep everybody out. I warned them. They came down in spite . . ."

"To enforce a court order." Williamson was inflexible. "You wounded my deputy too."

"I could have killed him. I hit him in the shoulder purposely, while he was trying to draw. He would have shot me and maybe some of these men."

"You can tell the judge about it." With Murdock well covered he turned to the crew. "Line up now and crawl up that ladder. We'll take you out through the mine."

"Wait a minute." Bishop showed his first protest. They had been working in a temperature over a hundred degrees, working in their undershirts. "Our clothes are back in the change room. We'll freeze if we go out like this."

"There'll be extra clothes in the Savage change room. They keep them for visitors."

The crew growled, but there were too many guns drawn against them. Bishop swore and began the climb and the others followed.

They were received in the Savage drift by posse members left up there, and marched toward the lift.

Murdock was the last of the tunnel men to go, with Williamson himself behind him, his gun still in his hand to show how much importance he placed on this particular prisoner.

The lift made three trips to haul them all, then they were herded into the change room. There were no coats.

Bishop began to argue and was slashed across the face by a deputy.

"Shut up."

There was a surge by the tunnel crew and for a moment a brawl was threatened, but mine police suddenly appeared in the doorways with short-barreled shotguns.

Bishop and Murdock were singled out, their hands tied behind their backs. The rest were left free, then all were marched into the street and toward the jail in a column of twos.

Murdock was still at the rear. It was bitter cold, below zero, with a cold wind blowing up over the divide. His thin cotton shirt, already damp with sweat, stuck to him. With his circulation cut by the rope around his wrists his fingers were soon icy numb. He thought they never would reach the side street that led to B and the courthouse.

The large room with the barred windows into which all except Murdock were shoved was unheated. Virginia had plenty of crime but most of it was petty, drunks, pickpockets, barroom fighters. They were normally held here only overnight. It was not equipped for longer occupation. Rows of benches along the wall offered the only place to sit or lie.

Bishop shouted at Williamson. "You promised us clothes. If there aren't any around here, send down to the tunnel office for our own."

"And get us a drink."

Murdock did not know who first yelled it, but it was taken up by every man in the cell.

"A drink. A drink. Alcohol will stop pneumonia."

"Shut up." The sheriff was furious. "No booze. You hoodlums are trouble enough without getting drunk too."

"We'll get sick and die in here."

But the prediction proved wrong. Their passage from the Savage had been noted by the street crowd, among them officials of the miners' union to which most of the tunnel workers belonged. The union had been a staunch friend of Sutro on the mountain and the individual members felt a closer bond with the crew than with their mine bosses.

The cell windows faced on both B and the side street that ran up at a sharp angle alongside the building. Within minutes both streets were crowded, faces pressing against the

121

windows. The prisoners raised the glass panes inside the bars. It was as cold in the room as in the street.

Men outside passed coats, sweaters, bottles of liquor through. The deputies tried to drive the crowd away but it kept growing. Both streets were choked, and Williamson saw that a mass eruption of violence was building and gave up.

The news spread in a lightning flash. Helen Powell heard it from a maid in her hotel room. The telegraph, now repaired, carried it to the town of Sutro. The tunnel workmen there called an emergency meeting in the wide street before the tunnel entrance, shouting, milling, threatening to arm themselves and march on Virginia. One agitator climbed to a barrel head, arms waving, drumming up a lust for vengeance.

Jack Bluett, sweating in spite of the cold, hauled him down and jumped up in his place. His reputation and his bull voice finally quieted the crowd enough so that he could be heard.

"Cool down. Knock it off. There's nothing to get in an uproar about. The boys are only being held for working against a court order. The charge isn't serious. They'll be released as soon as the judge is found, and we'll pay the fine."

Boris Stucki was just below him, shaking his fist and shouting. "What about Murdock? Shaw needed shooting. There's not a man on the mountain Buck Shaw hasn't hurrahed. Are we going to let them hang Murdock for that?"

Bluett did not like the crowd noise that rose again. He answered Stucki as if he were a mile away.

"We don't know yet just what happened, but I promise he'll get the best legal help we can find. Adolph Sutro and the rest of us will stand behind him every step."

It was not enough to satisfy them. There was a mood growing that demanded action, an immediate response. One determined group shoved toward the tunnel yelling for their fellows to follow, to get their hammers, single jacks, iron bars, to go on and up for an attack on the Savage.

Jack Bluett could not stop it alone. He jumped down and caught Stucki's arm.

"Go rout out the police. All of them. Throw a cordon around this mob and keep them corraled until they simmer down."

Stucki ran, and as he went, Bluett saw Sheldon drive in,

just returning from his trip to Virginia. He bulled through to him, shouted the news and watched Sheldon turn around and head up the mountain again.

The tunnel police erupted from the boarding house, running, slapping on their belts, drawing their guns, intercepting the wave of men as they crowded toward the tunnel, surrounding them. The men yelled, shook their fists, pushed ahead. Only when several shots were fired, kicking up dust at their feet, did they stop. But the urge to fight was too strong to be put down quickly. They stood in a packed group, arguing, some two hundred of them. Fist fights broke out among them, brief flurries of overflowing rage. The tunnel police had their hands full.

Jack Bluett had no time to stay and help. There was the bulkhead to protect. Bluett had fought the mineowners too long to have any doubt that they would take advantage of the situation and send a crew down to destroy it. He ran to the office, snatched a shotgun from the arms room, filled his pockets with shells and for once did not spare the mule that hauled the car he rode.

It was an eerie ride. Never in the years since the project had started had the work been completely stopped. The quiet was an ominous threat in itself.

And then ahead he heard sound. He left the car and ran. He came in sight of the bulkhead. Two men were there. What they were doing he could not tell. It was too far for an effective shot but he raised the gun and squeezed the trigger.

The roar filled and echoed through the tunnel. The men at the bulkhead jumped into the air and lit running. Bluett fired the second barrel to speed them, stopped to reload and went forward cautiously. They might be crouched along the dark wall, waiting for a shot at him.

There was no return fire. He passed the bulkhead and continued toward the jagged hole. He halted beside the tool-shed stoop, and his eyes fell on an open case of dynamite.

He went to it, cut three sticks into two sections each and fitted caps into the ends with two-foot lengths of fuse. He lined them up on top of a tool box with the fuses pointing toward him, then he lit one of his black, crooked cigars.

Afterward he squatted behind the tool box and fastened his eyes on the hole fifteen feet away.

He could hear the scrape of feet above, the mutter of voices. Then a man called.

"We've got a dozen guns up here. We're coming down. Throw in the sponge if you want to stay alive."

Bluett called, "And I've got some dynamite short-fused. Come ahead. There'll be a lot of meat splattered on the walls."

There was a low debate, then the answer. "I don't think you'd risk it. Gillette wouldn't like that."

Bluett clamped his cigar tight in his teeth, grinning. He eased around the box, ran silently forward, touching the fuse of one stick to the cigar coal. Then he tossed it in an arc, up into the dark hole, and ran for cover.

There was not enough explosive to blow the hole wider. There was enough to break chips loose and cascade them up. A chorus of yells came thin through the roar of the blast, then there was quiet.

Another short debate followed, then he heard hobnailed boots retreating along the mine drift. He went back and settled himself on the tool box. He would probably, he thought, be there a long time.

Chapter Eighteen

Boris Stucki, having turned out the tunnel police for the emergency duty, having watched them tumble down the stairs and empty out of the parlor, did not go with them. The big Russian was burning with a sullen frustration. Never in his life had he liked anyone as he liked Ken Murdock, and Murdock was going to get no help from any legal high jinks. Stucki had precious little faith in the justice of the courts. He stood in the parlor, considering what he could do. If he could sneak some of the tunnel men out of the cordon, they could ride up the hill and break Murdock out of the jail.

He was smiling over the idea when Sheila burst from her room wearing a fur hat and a heavy coat. Surprise made him blurt, "Where the hell are you going?"

She stopped, startled to see him still there. "To Virginia to see Ken. To let him know someone is behind him."

"A lot of us are that," he grinned. "You don't need to go. I'm just fixing to get some boys and go myself. We'll bust him loose and see he gets away free into the hills."

Her eyes widened and her breath rushed in. "Boris Stucki, don't you dare! That's the last thing in the world he should do. It would make him a fugitive for the rest of his life."

His mouth turned down. "Would you rather he hung?"

Her head shook violently. "They wouldn't do that. They couldn't. Buck Shaw drew first. Bryan told me Bishop said so."

"And Shaw worked for the mineowners. They take care of their own."

"Mr. Sutro wouldn't let it happen." She tried to sound certain but there was a sudden doubt in her tone.

Stucki grunted. "That's another reason they'll go after him hard. Ken works for Sutro. Anything they can do to make Sutro look bad helps them. I'm going up there."

She caught his arm, her fingers reaching only half around it. "Not tonight. Please. Not until we see what the court does. A Grand Jury has to decide whether he should even stand trial."

"Sure. Wait until they say he does. Then they'll have him so hid we can't even find him. Leave me go."

She stamped her foot. "Stucki, if you go I'm going with you."

"Oh, no you ain't."

"Then I'll go alone. I'll warn them."

He could hit her, knock her out. He could tie her up. But by the time he could get to Virginia someone would have found her and the crazy telegraph would probably be working and a posse would be waiting for him. He surrendered without grace.

"All right. Wait here. I'll go rent a buggy and get the boys."

Stucki could not get near the boys. The police had them blocked inside the tunnel, out of the cold. Indignantly he went for the buggy and the two went alone. He kept a sullen silence throughout the drive but Sheila pestered him with a running argument. Halfway up the grade they passed Sheldon going down. Stucki held his breath, but the man was so preoccupied with his own problems that he did not see them.

Sheldon had made a frantic effort to locate Judge Rising but the judge had had forewarning of the violence in the tunnel and chose not to be available. Sheldon then wired Sutro and waited in the telegraph room for the reply. It told him Sutro would arrive in Virginia the following evening. There being nothing more he could do on the mountain, Sheldon drove down to the lower town.

The mining camp that Stucki and Sheila Bryan drove into astonished them both. While C Street was unusually empty, B was jammed full. They could get nowhere near the court-house. But they could hear the joyous roistering inside the jail. So much liquor had been passed through the windows that the prisoners felt neither the cold nor any uneasiness about their situation. Listening on the outskirts of the mob, Stucki and Sheila learned that Ken Murdock was not in the big room. No one knew where he had been taken.

Ken Murdock was in fact in a solitary cell in the basement of the building. There was no light and it was as cold as the upstairs room. The thin straw mattress gave little protection and he shivered in the coat the deputies had flung him.

Unavoidably he heard the hilarity of the street crowd, the laughter and singing in the holding tank above his head. It helped him to sink deeper into a pool of hopeless despair.

He could not sleep. He lay reviewing his days in Washoe, his life since he had come south from Oregon, seeing himself as a perpetual outsider, a hick who would never be able to cope with the sophistries of Virginia City.

He blushed over his innocence about Helen Powell. He should have known in the beginning that there could never be anything between them. Even if she had not shown herself to be interested only in money, they had nothing at all in common. There was no bridge. In a rueful, backhanded way he was grateful to her, for she had opened to him experiences that he might otherwise never have known.

And Sutro. How flagrantly Sutro had used him. He and

126

Sheldon had paid him well, yes, but it was in their service that he had been forced to kill.

He did not regret that Shaw was dead. Having been the kind he was, Buck Shaw would probably have died by violence somewhere along the line. What Murdock resented was that it was he who had squeezed the trigger. The picture was vivid, the body crashing down, lying so quiet on the rock floor, the reverberations of the shot filling the station, the shock on the faces of the men around him. Murdock groaned, knowing that he would remember that moment for the rest of his life.

Helen Powell was not sleeping either. She sat at the table in her hotel room checking and rechecking figures on the papers before her. Her mouth made a bitter line and there was no beauty in her face. At last she rose, packed two suitcases, called a hack and directed the driver to take the cases to the station.

She did not ride the hack. She walked the almost empty length of C Street, hearing the dull roar around the courthouse on B. She let herself into the dark Powell brokerage office, drew the shades over the front windows, felt her way to the rear room, lighted a lamp and crouched before the big safe.

She spun the combination and pulled open the thick door. There was fifty thousand dollars inside, kept for emergencies that might arise after banking hours. She took out the large envelope, then spun up to her feet and dropped the envelope on the table as she heard the outside door open.

She thought of the little derringer that she had packed instead of carrying, wishing she had put it in her purse as she usually did. But there was not room in the bag for both the gun and the envelope. Her mind froze on the wish. She could not move.

Then the inner door opened and her uncle was there, leaning on his cane, wise eyes going from the envelope to the girl. His voice was tight, accusing.

"Helen, do you think this is wise?"

She knew that denial was fruitless. She spoke too quickly. "The show is over. That injunction will be made permanent. When the market opens on Monday the stock will hit bottom. They'll call for more margin. We can't pay any more. Let's get out with what cash we can salvage."

He continued to look at her and she said sharply, "Don't stand there. Get any papers you want. The train leaves at midnight."

He said slowly, "You expect me to go with you?"

"Why not? I was going to make sure of the money before I came for you."

The corner of his lip turned up. "Not from the figures I found in your room—after the desk clerk told me he hoped you would have a good trip."

"All right." She swept the air with her hands. "All right. I was going to go without you. But you're here, so come along. Remember, we've sold shares in other companies, shares we had held in our customer accounts, to meet our margin requirements. If we stay here we go to prison. If we're lucky we can reach San Francisco and get a ship before it's discovered that we've taken the cash. Fifty thousand isn't much, but it's better than prison."

Henry Powell had always lived by what he considered the code. But he was not a strong man. The prospect of prison sounded like a death sentence to him. He stood for a moment longer, irresolute, then he said quickly, "Bring the money. Let's go."

The girl snatched a paper and wrote a note to leave for the chief clerk. They were called away on business. They would return Tuesday night or Wednesday morning. If they could delay the search that long they should be able to get away.

Then they left the office, locking the door behind them. That was the last time either of the Powells was seen on the Comstock. Neither of them gave a thought to the cowboy in the cold cell.

Ken Murdock roused Sunday morning after a fitful, exhausted sleep. The crowd outside had dispersed, finally driven indoors by the bitter weather. The deputy who brought him a meager breakfast would give him no information. He sat through the day feeling completely cut off from the world.

Just after dark Sutro, Sheldon and the attorney were shown to the cell by the sheriff himself. Williamson might not like Sutro but the tunnel man was too popular with the bulk of the miners to be ignored.

When the sheriff left them alone with Murdock, Sutro was full of reassurances.

"We talked to the county attorney," he said. "They're taking you before the Grand Jury in the morning, asking for an indictment of first-degree murder."

Ken stared at him, shocked, only barely hearing as Sutro added, "This is Mr. Austin, our attorney, and he will be doing everything in his power to clear you."

Austin nodded, coughed for attention and as Ken looked toward him, said in a warning tone, "If I am to help you, son, you must tell me the exact truth. Did you kill Buck Shaw?"

Murdock nodded dumbly.

"Why? Precisely why?"

"Because he was drawing his gun. He was trying to kill me."

"Can you prove that he drew first? That you shot in self-defense?"

"He shot first. He missed and I fired before he could shoot a second time."

"Is there anyone to back up your story?"

"A lot of people. Bishop and his whole crew from the laterals. They were all there."

Sheldon gave a short, satisfied laugh. "That should settle it then."

But Austin cocked his head. "I'm not too sure there. They're employees of the tunnel company. The prosecution will claim they're prejudiced. And the fact that they're under arrest for contempt of court won't help."

"What kind of witnesses do you want?" Sheldon was getting red. "You think half of Virginia was down there watching?"

Austin tugged at his ear lobe, plainly dissatisfied.

Murdock said suddenly, "The deputy. The one I shot in the shoulder. He knows Shaw shot first."

The attorney's brows raised incredulously. "You surely don't expect him to testify *for* you, do you?"

Murdock opened his mouth to say, "He should, I could

have killed him." Then he did not. A bleak chill settled in him.

They went out, silent, misgiving heavy in the air, leaving Murdock even more lonely than he had been before they came. He stretched on the bunk, huddled the coat around him. But the cold came mostly from within.

A voice outside the cell said, "Hey, you, you still awake? You've got more visitors."

He sat up. The deputy had a lantern, and in its glow he had a dim view of two figures in the corridor. One was a woman. For the barest instant he thought it might be Helen Powell, but even as the thought crossed his mind his new, hard-won awareness told him that was impossible. Then he recognized Stucki and knew that the girl wrapped in the heavy coat was Sheila Bryan.

Suddenly he did not want to see her, did not want her to come into the cell. He was acutely conscious of what she had said about carrying a gun. He remembered her disdain at his getting drunk. If she said "I told you so," he felt that he would throw her out.

She did not say it. She did not say anything, hardly looked at him as she followed Stucki into the cell.

The jailer locked the door and set the lantern on the corridor floor to leave a little light coming through the bars. He said, "Five minutes," and went away.

Murdock was on his feet. He motioned the girl to a seat on the bunk, but she did not move.

Stucki said, "You all right?"

"As good as can be expected. How come they let you in?"

Stucki showed his big teeth. "Ten bucks. That deputy ain't above liking a drink. We tried to come last night but there wasn't a chance."

Murdock looked from him to the girl. "You've been up here since last night?"

She spoke for the first time. "I stayed with friends."

Stucki was not going to be cut out of the conversation. "I wanted to get some boys and bust you out. She wouldn't let me. Objected to your being a fugitive from now on."

She raised her eyes and met his, unsmiling. He knew that she watched to see his reaction.

130

"She's right," he said without hesitation. "A man might as well be dead as on the run for the rest of his life."

Stucki blew out his breath. "You ain't never hanged before."

Sheila made a wordless sound of protest. The Russian ignored her.

"Well, pal, we'll wait and see what the court says, then we'll decide. When do you go before it?"

"Sutro was just here."

"We saw him come out. We waited for him to get clear. What did he say?"

"That they'll take me before the Grand Jury tomorrow morning."

"What's that mean?"

Murdock was not exactly clear. "I think they have to decide whether the evidence is strong enough to take me to trial."

"What about the lawyer? What's he think?"

Murdock scuffed at the stone floor with his boot toe. "He didn't sound very hopeful. Said Bishop and the crew would be considered prejudiced witnesses and wouldn't be believed."

"But there were other people there." It was a cry from the girl.

Murdock shrugged. "Only the deputy I shot in the shoulder. They'd believe him, but the lawyer thinks he wouldn't testify. He should though."

"Why should he?" Stucki was as skeptical as Austin had been.

"Well, I could have killed him when he went for his gun. I didn't. I figured he was doing his job. I'd never seen him before—hadn't anything against him—" his voice trailed off. His action had been instinctive. There hadn't been time for reason as he was making it sound.

The jailer's footsteps stopped their talk. He picked up the lantern and came on to unlock the door.

"Get a move on." His voice was urgent. "The sheriff's liable to come back any minute. If he catches you here it's my job."

Chapter Nineteen

On Monday morning virtually all business in Virginia was at a standstill. The town had not been so generally roused since the last great fire. Crowds formed early around the courthouse, but the Grand Jury session was closed. Only those directly concerned were admitted to the building.

Stucki and Sheila stood at the edge of the pack with a group of tunnel men who had come up the hill. They saw Gillette go inside, flanked by the mine's attorneys. They saw Sutro and Sheldon go in with their legal staff. The prosecutor, then the jurymen were piloted through the jam. After that they waited.

Inside, Murdock sat with Austin, Sutro and Sheldon. He studied the jury as the men took their places in the box. None of them looked like miners. The Grand Jury had been selected from the businessmen, the bankers, the leaders of the town. He tried to listen but he did not actually hear what the prosecutor said as he outlined the evidence. Dully he heard Gillette testify, and the sheriff tell of the injunction and of the deputy's trying to enforce it.

Then Austin put him on the stand and was asking what to Murdock sounded like ridiculously obvious questions.

"You are employed by the tunnel company as a guard?"

"That's right."

"And on Saturday you were as usual posted at the point where there is an opening between the Savage mine and the tunnel?"

He nodded.

"Speak up, please, so the jury can hear you."

"I was on guard. We kept a guard at the breakthrough twenty-four hours a day."

"Why was such a guard maintained?"

"Because Mr. Sutro was afraid the Savage people would try to destroy our bulkhead."

"And why is this bulkhead so important?"

"Because the mineowners had been threatening to pump the hot waste water from their sumps into the tunnel. If they did that before we were prepared for it the tunnel could be ruined."

"Did you have orders to shoot anyone who tried to enter the tunnel from the mine?"

Murdock stole a glance at Sutro, at Sheldon. Their faces were blank. He could not tell what went on in their minds.

"I was told to keep them out."

"By force if necessary?"

He nodded again, then realizing that he had to speak out for the record, he said, "That's right."

"And when the deputy and Shaw came down, who first drew a gun?"

"Shaw did. He meant to kill me. I could see it in his eyes."

The attorney, his eyes on the jury, said, "That is all," and walked away.

Murdock felt helplessly exposed in the chair as the prosecutor came forward. He was a tall man with a long horse face, and eyes that held Murdock's in a hypnotic lock. The voice held a repugnance, as if he were debased by talking to the prisoner.

"Is it not true, Mr. Murdock, that you had had gun trouble with Buck Shaw before Saturday?"

Ken swallowed to ease the tightness in his throat. "Yes, sir."

"What started it?"

"Well, he attacked Mr. Sheldon in a saloon on the night I first got to Virginia. I took the guns away from him and the men with him."

"I see. What was his reaction?"

"He threatened me."

"So when Mr. Shaw went into the tunnel on Saturday, you pulled your gun and fired and killed him."

"No, sir." Ken was urgent. "He drew first. He fired first. I shot in self-defense."

"You killed him, Mr. Murdock. And the only people who saw you do it are, like yourself, employees of the tunnel company."

Trying to answer the questions quietly, watching the jury,

Murdock knew sickeningly that he was not believed. Even Sutro's attorney Austin seemed to doubt him. Dutifully he called Bishop, but the prosecutor successfully discredited his testimony, making much of his not unbiased position and his friendship for Murdock.

It became plain to everybody that Ken Murdock would be held over for trial. The decision was on their faces as the room was ordered cleared so that the jury could begin its deliberation. Murdock was already on his feet, being led out, when the door was pushed open and a voice called over the heads of the guards there.

"Wait a minute, please."

Everyone looked that way. A man stood in the entrance. His right shoulder was thickly bandaged and a woman in a nurse's uniform hovered close to him.

The jury foreman who had conducted the hearing said in annoyance, "What do you want?"

"I have some testimony to give."

"Who are you?"

"Deputy Sheriff Stan Thomas."

Murdock had not recognized him. He had seen the man only once, in the uncertain light of the tunnel, and from the way the morning had gone the appearance seemed only suspect.

The foreman, the prosecutor, Austin were also suspicious as Thomas walked down the aisle. No one knew what he was going to say or whether they wanted to hear him. He took the stand without invitation.

Thomas had been a witness in other cases and although this was a hearing, not a trial, he knew how to conduct himself. The foreman asked the questions.

"You were summoned to the Savage on Saturday because the tunnel crew was heard blasting in spite of the restraining order served on them?"

"Yes. Sheriff Williamson wasn't in town when the call came, so I went. I had nobody to take with me, so Mr. Gillette loaned me some mine police."

"You did not object to that?"

"Why should I? I needed some backing up, I figured, and Shaw knew his way around underground. I didn't."

"Well, what is your testimony?"

134

"We went down into the tunnel. I said who I was. Murdock told us to go back up. Shaw drew his gun and fired. Then Murdock shot him."

The prosecutor was now shouting to be heard. The foreman refused him, demanding order, finally getting it and turning back to Thomas.

"You are certain Shaw drew his gun first?"

"Not only drew but fired before Murdock's gun was out of its holster."

"Would you say Shaw was trying to kill Murdock?"

The deputy looked at him in pity. "You don't pull a gun on an armed man unless you mean to kill him. That's suicide."

The prosecutor shouted again, this time making himself heard over the increasing babble in the room.

"Are you a friend of Murdock?"

The deputy touched his shoulder but did not mention it.

"I don't know him at all."

"And he wounded you at the time he killed Shaw. What are you getting for coming out of the hospital to do this?"

Deputy Stan Thomas's eyes turned to frost, his mouth to a thin line.

"He wounded me when he could have killed me. Because in the heat of the moment I was going for my own gun. I came here because I heard he was accused of murder. It was not murder. It was self-defense. As other witnesses must have told you."

Ken Murdock was confused. Thomas barely glanced at him as he left with the nurse. The room was cleared of all except the jury. When the others had gone, his lawyer and two guards led him out, Austin shaking his head, saying, "You are the luckiest man I ever heard of. I didn't call that deputy because I thought the last thing he'd do would be testify for you."

Murdock's first interest was not Thomas. He said anxiously, "Does it mean I'll be freed?"

"I don't see what else they can do. They surely can't claim he's prejudiced in your favor."

Ten minutes later the jury proclaimed a verdict of justifiable homicide. Ken Murdock was cleared, but not yet freed. Judge Rising was trying the crews arrested for contempt of court. Murdock was led to the second-floor courtroom and seated with the defendants there. Sutro, Sheldon and the legal staff, Gillette and the Savage lawyers had moved up too.

On the stand Sheriff Williamson told of serving the writ on Bishop. Gillette testified that Savage miners in the deep drifts had heard blasts and guessed that the tunnel men were still working. The wounded deputy and three of the mine police who said they had gone to the breakthrough with him said they had found the tunnel work going on.

The shooting was not mentioned. The Grand Jury had already ruled on that.

Rising sat hunched in his chair peering over his steel rimmed spectacles at the defendants.

Sheldon was called and asked why he had ignored the writ. He countered in a careful tone that it had been improperly served. Instead of serving on the employed workmen, Williamson should have driven down to Sutro and served it on the officers. He explained that he had tried to telegraph Virginia for verification and because the instrument was dead had gone in search of the judge or the sheriff.

After two hours of bickering, Rising ruled that since Sheldon had not been served personally he was not in contempt, but that Bishop, who had received the writ and then willfully ignored the court order, was. Rising fined Bishop one hundred dollars and dismissed the rest of the crew.

Cheers filled the courtroom. Rising rapped angrily for order. When it was restored the clerk announced that arguments would be heard as to why the injunction should not be made permanent.

The tunnel attorney explained at some length the effect on the tunnel should the mine sumps be diverted before the drainage ditch was finished and sealed to prevent the water and steam from flooding the main haulage way.

Rising listened with closer attention than he had to Sheldon before. He questioned Gillette and the Savage representatives. When they had finished he dismissed the injunction. The case was closed.

Gillette's eyes bugged. He rose to protest but his attorney caught his arm, forced him toward the corridor where the spectators were shoving toward the street.

Gillette was furious. Rising had been known in Virginia as

a mine judge. Ever since mining began along the Comstock the Lode had been wracked by law suits, and the judges were sardonically classified as to whether their findings favored the mineowners or not.

"You know what I think?" Gillette stopped on the steps, his voice a hoarse whisper. "I think he sold out."

The attorney did not argue. Privately he had felt from the beginning that unless they had a mine judge they had no grounds on which the injunction should be made permanent. But he did not say so.

"What are you going to do now?"

The superintendent was breathing noisily through his nose. "Wire San Francisco. See what they want done."

He sent a long message and waited impatiently in his office. Two hours later he had his answer, in code.

"Start the pumps. Empty the sumps into the tunnel before they can close the bulkhead."

Chapter Twenty

They streamed out of the courthouse into the mob of the curious that still filled B Street. The tunnel crew was noisy with exuberance, sure that they had beaten the mineowners. Some of them had caught colds but there had been enough free liquor in the jail to make even those consider this a holiday.

Murdock saw Sheila beside Boris Stucki's big frame beyond the edge of the crowd and shoved through to them. The girl watched him, quiet, but Stucki grinned and clapped him on the back.

"Where you been? We heard the jury turned you loose an hour ago."

"They held me for the contempt of court hearing."

Sheila said quickly, "What did they do about that?"

"The judge threw out the injunction. He fined Bishop a hundred dollars and dismissed the charges against the rest of us. A lucky thing—that deputy I shot came and testified for me or I'd have been up for murder."

"No luck about it." Stucki winked broadly at the girl.

"Hush," she said tightly.

There was a short silence while Murdock looked from one to the other, then Stucki grunted.

"If she won't tell you, I will. That deputy didn't just hop out of bed and come on his own . . ."

"Stucki, stop it."

The Russian held the girl at arm's length, his grin widening.

"Sheila hauled me to the hospital and bulled her way in. They weren't going to let us see him but she said we were his brother and sister. She jumped all over him, said you'd risked your own life by hitting his shoulder instead of killing him. She said if he didn't tell the truth in court she'd tell every miner on the mountain and they'd make it too hot for him ever to work in Virginia again."

The girl's eyes were on the stones of the street and color flamed in her cheeks, but Stucki paid no attention.

"Boy," he said, "she'd put a Philadelphia lawyer to shame. She was like a she-bear fighting for her cub. If you don't marry her, I'll break your fool neck."

With a sharp cry Sheila darted off into the crowd. She was fast, running down the steep hill toward C Street. She almost reached the corner before they caught her.

"Sheila—wait." Murdock snagged her wrist. "Give me a chance to say thanks, won't you?"

She turned stricken eyes up to him. "Stucki had no right saying that. I don't want to marry you. I didn't do it for— I'd have done it for any of the boys."

He had the sense not to say anything, only held her arm and the three of them climbed on to the livery.

They made the long drive down the mountain in constrained silence. Even Stucki, normally the most talkative man at the boarding house, had nothing to say. Not until they turned up Tunnel Avenue toward the barn and saw a crowd around the tunnel portal. Then his good humor returned.

"The boys must have heard the news and got up a celebration."

But Murdock stiffened. "What's that behind them? Smoke."

The recurring fires that had plagued the mines had given smoke a special terror throughout the Lode district. Murdock whipped the horse forward, pulled up just short of the fringe of the men, looped the lines around the whip socket and jumped down. Stucki went off the far side as Murdock gave the girl a hand, then they ran together, calling ahead.

"What is it?"

The men nearest them turned, their faces strained. "Water. The Savage is pumping the sumps through the break."

They saw then that it was steam, not smoke, rolling out of the tunnel mouth, hiding the headframe. Murdock located Jack Bluett beside the office, talking to Al Temple, and broke a way toward them with Sheila and Stucki at his heels.

Bluett caught sight of them and his face relaxed a little. "Murdock. When did you get here?"

"Just now. They turned me loose."

"I know. Sheldon wired us."

"When did this start?"

"Only a few minutes ago. As soon as I got the wire that the injunction was dismissed I sent a crew inside. They're mostly still there. So are the mules—" he slammed a fist into his palm. "God damn Gillette's gang."

Murdock said, "Maybe they didn't think anyone was in there, didn't realize you knew the injunction was lifted."

"They knew. They don't care. It's part and parcel of the way they've always fought us. They know we had them licked. That injunction was their last gasp. Now they want to wreck the tunnel. The finished section of ditch is taking the water, but back behind it the stinking stuff is already six, eight inches deep on the floor. Hot as it is, if it gets in behind the timbering it will wash out the clay and collapse the walls. And there go all the years—all the work."

"The bulkhead." Murdock estimated the headroom beneath the roiling steam. "We can still get through and close it."

"You and who else?" Bluett was bitter. "You can't do it alone and nobody will go."

Temple said quickly, "I'd go to hell before I'd go in there. It would be a lot cooler."

139

Sheila Bryan caught at Murdock's shirt. "He's right, Ken. Don't go. Not you—oh, not you." Her voice was a wail.

He shook free, not seeing how her tone jarred Temple, giving her a wry smile.

"Don't forget I've got stock in this tunnel. If it's ruined I'll never get my money back. Stucki, you going with me?"

The big Russian rolled his eyes. Then he hitched his pants and spat. "If you're damn fool enough, I guess I got to. Can't have you lick me and then put me down too."

Sheila Bryan swung wildly on Temple. "Al, you can't let them go in there alone . . ."

The blond man looked down on her, wetting his lips. Then he lifted and dropped his shoulders in futility. "What the hell. What difference does it make?"

Murdock raised his voice. "We need more. A couple of husky men. Those doors are heavy."

Boris Stucki might no longer be Chief but he was still a force to reckon with. His eyes went over the circle of men, settled on a yellow-haired giant, then a man built like a gorilla.

"You, Schwartz, and you, Donovan. You going to let those men in there boil because you're scared? Best thing in the world to clean your pores in a steam bath. Come on."

They yelled an obscenity, then they were running behind Murdock toward the change room, the lamp room.

They rode a mule car back to the point beyond which the drain ditch was still open. Until then the layer of steam clung against the ceiling, leaving them a clear passage. From there on a sluggish river of thick, vile-smelling waste fluid covered the floor, pouring into the open mouth of the ditch.

They left the car, Murdock in the lead, and jumped to the top of the wooden box through which the air pipes ran back to the faces. It was not waterproof, designed only to protect the pipes from damage, but the lid was solid and six inches above the flood level.

In the beginning the sump water had cooled somewhat in its long course. As they went deeper, wisps of steam coiled up from it, and then it rose in a cloud. It and the increasing heat made breathing hard. They tied handkerchiefs over their noses and mouths. The lamps became of less and less help, the light reflecting back from the thickening moisture in the air.

Men loomed out of the fog running toward them along the pipe box. They squeezed by carefully, balancing to keep from falling into the deepening flood. The black, moving surface glittered under the wall lamps with the ugly, sinuous flow of a hunting python.

The men they passed were unhurt. The mules were not so fortunate, splashing blindly through the steaming soup, their brays of pain filling the tunnel with the despair of hell.

The foreman of the crew was the last to materialize out of the gloom. He squinted at Murdock through reddened, swollen eyes.

"Where the hell you going?"

"The bulkhead. Your crew all safe? Nobody left inside?"

"All safe. No thanks to those mine bastards. There wasn't any warning. We were getting set to drill when the water hit us. We didn't know where it was coming from until we got out of the lateral, then we saw it coming through the bulkhead. You can't close it now. You'd better get out."

"We're going to close it." Murdock maneuvered past the man.

"You'll never make it, I tell you. There's too much water. You can't move the doors against the pressure."

Stucki, embracing him as if in a dance, said, "There's a way. Get on clear."

They went on, into deepening density, passing two more mules. These stood, the hot water swirling around their legs that were cooked through, braying their agony.

"Shoot them, for God's sake," Murdock called to Temple, the only one with a gun.

The tunnel had never seemed so long. At any moment he expected to see the masonry walls of the bulkhead take shape through the steam. At one point a dam of floating tool boxes and debris, jammed against an ore car, backed up a pool that flowed over the top of the pipe box. There they waded, feeling for footing. Their heavy underdrawers, socks, pants, thick boots, protected them there, but some of the heat soaked through.

Then, almost close enough to touch it, the dark shape of the fitted stone bulwark was there. Behind it the steam was almost a solid, and through that came the pounding splash of falling water.

Murdock knew the structure intimately. His mind's eye saw every detail. Embedded into the rock walls on either side, the masonry jutted toward the center of the tunnel bore. The two openings were separated by a middle column some four feet wide. The frames of the openings were slanted, were larger on the upstream side than on the down. The doors were shaped to match, to nest into the frames and wedge there. Above the frames a solid stone header closed in the space to the ceiling.

The doors were hung on great wrought-iron strap hinges and were kept swung back on the upstream side, against the bulkhead itself.

On the door faces and on the stone jambs were iron brackets near the top and bottom to receive horizontal iron bars, a precaution against any possibility that the doors might somehow be sucked out of their nests by any freak current as water built up behind them.

To close these doors now it was necessary to wade into the steaming water, nearly a foot deep now, gushing through the openings, and force the three-foot-thick pine slabs out against the current's pressure, pivot them on their hinges until the pressure should drive them into the jambs.

The first door was not too hard. Schwartz and Donovan, with Stucki, sloshed through the rushing sluice, got a grip on the free edge and pulled it outward until Stucki could work in behind the slab. Putting his back to the masonry for leverage, Stucki pushed as the others pulled. The door gave grudgingly, swung on its hinges, passed the right angle point. The current then slammed it shut.

Murdock was splashed with burning hot water but ignored it, dropping the top iron bar into the brackets as Al Temple set the lower one. The other three men stumbled through the second opening, fighting toward the pipe box. All five swung up onto that, dancing on it as the steaming water sent its heat in to sear their legs. They waited there until they cooled enough to make the second attempt.

The first method would not work this time because of the danger that someone would be trapped on the upstream side. With one door closed, the water behind was building up faster, the torrent coming through had become a chute. If someone were caught there would be no possibility of opening the door to rescue him.

When they dared step into the water again, Murdock brought a rope from the tool alcove that served that area and swung a loop, tossing it to drop over the bracket at the free end of the door. He snubbed it up, then tossed the line over the matching bracket on the center column. All five then hauled on the rope, but even with the combined strength they could not swing the door out from the wall against the current.

Al Temple was cursing tonelessly. "We'll never make it. Let's get the hell out of this steam tank before we cook."

Murdock would not give up. "There's got to be a way," he insisted, and climbed again to the pipe box. "Let's think about it."

They were all willing enough to get out of the water again, standing on one foot, waving the other for what little cooling effect that had. It was Donovan who made the next suggestion.

"If we could pull the hinge pins," he said, "maybe we could tip the door over, get it flat in the water and then work it around square with the opening and tip it up with the ropes."

It was worth a try, Murdock thought. He thrashed across the flood to the tool alcove again, found another rope, a drill with a slender bit, and a hammer. While Stucki held the bit tip against the bottom of the lower hinge pin, Murdock used the hammer. The pin gave, slid up and Murdock pulled it.

They began working on the upper pin. The door canted a fraction and the pin bound. Donovan wormed in beside Stucki, put his shoulder to the door edge to force it back, and Murdock's next hammer blow sent the pin flying free. It arced through the air and hit Al Temple in the face. Temple swore viciously at Murdock.

With the door now unattached they got a rope on the top bracket and with all of them pulling were able to tip the door, drop it on its side against the opening. That blocked the water from coming through for the moment, but they had still to turn it on its back, swing it square and lift the top.

The pressure behind it then could be counted on to slam it up into position.

Working with crowbars pushing against the bottom, with two men holding the top to keep it from falling the wrong way, they slowly moved it. With the force of the chute now more widely distributed, the door flattened down into the water, and the water again poured through, over and under it.

Murdock jumped on it as if it were a raft, balancing on its face to keep it from upending again. The flood was now above the men's knees, stinging the flesh of their legs. They could not tolerate it much longer. Neither could they stop working or all they had gained would be lost.

Stucki, Donovan and Schwartz plunged their hands into the steaming flood, caught the door edge and pivoted it so that its bottom edge came against the opening. It came in a rush, hit the masonry hard. It knocked Murdock off his balance and sent him stumbling, off the door and through the opening. He came up with a crashing jar against Al Temple.

Temple's nerves were already on a ragged edge. He had watched Sheila, outside, blast his last hope of winning her. It was Murdock's safety, not his that had wrung the protest from her. He had been frightened of coming in here and been forced to come or forfeit his place among men of Murdock's, even Stucki's caliber. He had been hit in the face by an iron pin driven by Murdock.

He reacted without thought. As Murdock was thrown against him, he staggered back, balled his fist and swung with all his strength, a looping blow that chopped down on the back of Murdock's neck. He swung the other hand, up, against Murdock's chin.

Murdock fought to keep from falling, stunned by the suddenness, the unexpectedness of the attack. He wrapped his arms around Temple, hanging on, and they stood swaying, the hot water rushing around their thighs.

He had captured only one of Temple's arms, and the blond man in his blind rage was hammering blows on Murdock's shoulder, on his head. In a nightmare daze he knew that he must stop Temple. They could not stand here and fight in this blistering flood. There was no time left to try to shout reason into the man.

144

Murdock let go his hold, backed a step and swung from his heels. His fist traveled a foot and shocked against Temple's neck just below his ear.

Al Temple flailed back, splashing, already falling, his backward steps unable to keep pace with his upper body. He went down, arching back. His head hit the edge of the pipe box and knocked him out. He twisted, going into the water on his face, and floated, his arms and legs limp.

The flow of the water was as strong as ever, as deep. Temple's body swung with the current, being carried downstream. As if Murdock's mind was two minds on two different problems at the same time, he snapped a glance back at the doorway.

The panel was not in place yet. Stucki stood on the near end of it, trying to keep it from lifting as the water gushed under it. If that end went up first, the door would be backward, would not nest. Donovan and Schwartz had the ropes set, around the upper door brackets and over the brackets in the top of the frame, to give the upward leverage needed to swing the panel up. Both were in the water, leaning against the ropes, their shoulder muscles knotted as they strained. But a thick sheet of water still ran over the face of the door.

Then Murdock was diving after Temple, throwing himself headlong, swimming with powerful strokes of his arms and using his legs as pistons thrusting against the tunnel floor. The hot water seared through his shirt and blistered his hands.

Then he had caught one of Temple's boots, pulled it back and tangled his fingers in the man's shirt collar. He hauled the face out of the water, dragged the unresisting body to the pipe box and with a spurt of strength born of desperation rolled Temple up to its dry top. Then he sat down on the planking and was barely able to swing his own legs out of the stinking stew.

He gritted his teeth against the burning that continued inside his boots, squeezing his eyes shut to keep from crying out.

It surprised him when a hand dropped on his shoulder. He opened his eyes. Stucki was there, and Donovan and Schwartz, in a mad dance on the box top to relieve their own pain.

For a second Murdock thought they had abandoned the job, given up. Then he looked past them. The door was up. It was properly nested. The cross bars were dropped in the brackets to hold it. And the water was stopped. It would now build higher and higher behind the bulkhead, press the door even tighter, until the steaming level overflowed into the Savage drift or the mine crew shut off their pumps.

He turned to examine Al Temple. The man was breathing, beginning to moan. Murdock started to get to his feet, to lift him, to carry him out of the tunnel. He could not stand.

Stucki shoved him down, saying, "Rest awhile. We all need it. Wait until the water goes down. It's easier walking on the floor than up here."

Murdock nodded, unable to waste breath on talk. He wondered if he would make the trip alive. He wasn't sure.

The water subsided quickly, running off down the slight slant of the tunnel, and the swirling steam went with it. It was still hotter than Ken had ever known it in here, but even the small drop in temperature was a great relief. They waited until only a thin trickle slewed between the iron rails, then they began walking.

They all limped painfully, their feet blistered, nearly boiled. Stucki, Donovan, Schwartz took turns carrying Temple. The blond man was barely conscious, unresisting. Murdock, without their years of mine labor to develop and harden the muscles on their big frames, dragged behind them, fighting total exhaustion.

Ahead of them they heard calls, their names being shouted in spaced repetition. Then there were lights coming toward them. They stopped and dropped down to rest in the muck left on the floor.

Jack Bluett came up with more men and a mule car. With the water down, the animal could again walk between the tracks. Temple was loaded into the car and the others climbed in. Murdock was too tired to register what Bluett said. Before the mule was unhitched and led to the other end of the car, he was asleep.

Chapter Twenty-One

Even when they are not medically serious, burns are most painful injuries. All five of the men who had closed the bulkhead suffered. Al Temple was in the worst shape. Floating in that water as he had, his face, hands, stomach swelled with bloated blisters. When his boots were cut off, his legs were angry red, streaked with blisters where the water had seeped inside the boots.

Murdock's face was a little better than Temple's but his hands were equally scalded and around his belt line the water trapped against him within his shirt raised a fluid-filled welt. His torso looked like a boiled lobster. The other three had all but parboiled legs and hands but their bodies escaped much damage.

They were taken to the boarding house where Sheila Bryan established a single room as a hospital. Doctor Brierly arrived as their clothes were being cut away with scissors, bringing a gallon of carron oil. Jack Bryan and Bluett helped, pouring the soothing mix of lime water and linseed oil over the burns, not daring to spread it with their hands for fear of breaking the great blisters.

Murdock did not sleep the first part of that first night but lay with his nerve ends twitching, his skin feeling frozen. Al Temple moaned with every breath. Stucki and Donovan cursed in a long monotone. Schwartz endured the ordeal in a grim, patient silence. After midnight Brierly came again. The emergency had caught him with his stock of morphine at a low. He had raced to Virginia for more, and as he administered it and the drug took hold, the room slowly quieted. The men slept, out of pain for the first time in hours.

For two days neither Temple nor Murdock could tolerate food. By the third the vice grip of pain began to subside in Murdock and his numb mind turned away from his body. He lay watching Sheila, who spent most of the hours in the room.

She hovered over Temple, still the most critical, with a

147

gentleness she had never shown before. Murdock reacted with a rising of the forlorn sensation that had made him so alone throughout his first days here.

Unconsciously he compared Sheila with Helen Powell, and the broker lost whatever illusion there had been left. He could not visualize Helen nursing anyone, soiling her hands with messy emulsions or mothering such men as these crude laborers. If he had known that she and her uncle were on a ship bound for the Sandwich Islands it would have meant nothing to him now.

Stucki, Donovan and Schwartz were healing quickly, showing the restlessness of active men. Stucki was worst, insisting on getting up until Sheila threatened to throw him out of the house. Like a sulky little boy he compromised, sitting on the edge of his bed talking across to Murdock.

"The hell with this job. What about that ranch of yours? When you get it back, how about giving me a job? I don't know a cow from a horse, but I've got a strong back."

"Sure." Murdock's voice was dull. "If I get it back." He had about given up hope and oddly he found that he did not care. The ranch would be a very empty place without the people he had met at the tunnel. Without Sheila. The knowledge came as an unhappy flash.

She was sitting beside Al Temple, reading to him as he lay with a cloth soaked in carron oil draped loosely over his face. Her voice was so low that it barely carried across the room. Murdock's eyes went to her and anchored there.

Stucki watched Murdock. Twice the Russian opened his mouth to speak. Twice he closed it, thinking better about what he had intended to say.

He was drawing a breath to try again when the door opened and Sheldon came in. Bluett had visited them every day but Sheldon had not come before.

The superintendent went to Temple first, knowing that his injuries were the most severe. They could not hear what he said but he put a hand on the bandaged shoulder lightly. Then he came to stand between Stucki and Murdock.

"Miss Bryan says you're giving her trouble, you won't stay down." He was talking to Stucki.

Stucki grinned. "Why the hell should I stay in bed for a few blisters?"

Sheldon laughed and turned to Murdock, but Stucki wasn't through.

"What's with this guy Sutro? Bluett's been here and now you, but we ain't heard a peep out of Sutro. It was his tunnel we saved."

"He knows," Sheldon said. "You'll hear when he's got some news for you."

Stucki showed his doubt in a grunt. "Where is he?"

"In San Francisco dickering with the mine men."

"There's nothing new in that."

Sheldon's face creased in a quick smile. "This time, yes. When they pumped the sumps into the tunnel it backfired. The bulkhead stopped it and it overflowed into the mine. Before they found out it was happening and shut down the pumps, the lower levels were flooded so they couldn't be worked. It will take weeks before it all drains into the sumps again and meanwhile more water is seeping in. They need the tunnel like they never did before."

"Then why are they still dickering?"

"Still trying to cut Sutro's price. I'll let you know as soon as the deal is made."

It was made ten days later. All of them, even Temple, were up although Sheila was still riding herd, not allowing them to put boots on their tender feet nor go to work with the thin skin so new on their hands. The edginess of cabin fever was beginning to infect them and Murdock made a point of staying out of Temple's way. The man had apologized for his wild attack but his tone told that resentment still had a hold on him.

In the long-awaited contract Sutro did compromise on his price. The tunnel would handle ore that milled at forty dollars a ton or less for a dollar a ton, and the richer ores for two dollars. They would finish the drain ditch in ninety days. The mines also compromised, agreeing to advance seventy dollars a foot to drive the laterals that would connect their mines with the main tunnel.

The news swept the Lode. At the bottom of the mountain, Sheldon brought it first to the boarding house. Impromptu celebrations flowered. Stucki, Donovan and Schwartz would stay indoors no longer. In several layers of heavy socks in

149

lieu of boots, they erupted out of the house to join the parading crews.

Sheila brought home still other news. Sutro was going to give a mammoth party at his mansion in Sutro town. The five men who had closed the bulkhead were to be the honored guests.

Ken Murdock thought ahead with a sinking heart. He could not go. He could not spend a night watching Sheila and Al Temple laughing together, dancing together. Knowing was bad enough, but seeing it would shut her completely away from him. He used the first excuse he could think of.

"I don't have the right clothes."

Her eyes widened in astonishment. "You've got that suit you bought with your first paycheck."

He squirmed, grasping for the reaction he had seen the night he went to dinner with Helen Powell.

"It's not—it's not the kind of clothes people wear at the International Hotel."

"Ken Murdock. Sutro isn't interested in your clothes. What do you think Stucki and the others have to wear?"

"I know, but I wouldn't feel easy."

She folded her fists on her hips. "Well, if it's good enough for me to be seen with, it's good enough for you to wear."

For a minute he did not understand. Then he did not believe what he thought he heard.

"You—you with me?"

"Don't you want me with you?"

"But—But—of course I do—but Al Temple is going and I thought . . ."

"What's he got to do with it?"

He fumbled. "Well—the way you took care of him—like he was special . . ."

"I took care of you too, didn't I?"

"Yes—but not in the same way."

"You." Her eyes half closed. "Are you jealous of Al Temple?"

He wanted to deny it. He choked trying. Then he said in a sheepish voice, "I guess so. Yes."

The smile that spread over her face was slow, like a sunrise. "That's the nicest thing you ever said to me. It was worth waiting for. I thought you'd never . . ."

150

He was kissing her. He did not know exactly how it had happened. He was clumsy with inexperience but she seemed not to notice, to have little experience herself, and instinct guided them.

Finally she pushed him away, needing to get her breath. "Whooo . . ."

He tried to pull her back into the circle of his arms but she ducked around the kitchen table.

"Just take it a little easy, Ken. There'll be plenty of time afterward."

He stalked her, his head spinning. "After what?"

Obliquity was not in her. She was as direct as a shot.

"After we're married. When it will mean something."

He stared at her blankly as two thoughts hit him at the same time. The word *marriage* crystallized for him the growing emotion that had kept him so unhappy these past two weeks. Also crystallized was the brutal knowledge that he had nothing at all to offer her that she would accept.

She misread his face and backed away, stiffening, aghast that she had spoken, her cheeks flaming.

"I'm sorry. I shouldn't have—Ken, you don't have to marry me . . ."

"Sheila." It was a high sound, wrung from him. He jumped for her, caught her, lest she should run away as she had so many times before. "I want to. I want you. But how can we? You said you wouldn't marry a gun guard . . ."

She shook her head.

The ranch had been lost to him for so long, was still so far out of reach that it did not even enter his head now. His voice came hollow.

"I haven't got anything else. I can't support you on the forty a month a rider gets."

She came against him, wrapped her arms around him, pressed her face against his chest.

"I don't care. Don't think about that now. Let's go to the party. Let's have tonight. Tomorrow we can worry about what to do."

They went to the party. Many of the tunnel people and local officials they knew were there. There were hundreds of people they did not know.

This was the high moment for Adolph Sutro and he was

151

making the most of it. He had won his long and bitterly fought gamble, and the taste of victory was sweet. He welcomed his guests with the air of a prince regent, but he was apparently as glad to see the lowest mucker from the tunnel as he was the governor of the state or the mine superintendents who had grudgingly accepted his invitation.

Even the weather favored Sutro. A midseason gap in the winter brought a flow of warm air up from the lower desert and the party was staged outdoors. The grounds were gaily lighted with colored paper lanterns. Food and refreshments were set on long tables sparkling with snowy linen, silver, crystal. White-coated waiters hurried with trays among the crowd.

Ken Murdock openly gawked. The scene was a fairyland outside his imagination. Sheila was as overwhelmed as he but she hid her uncertainty better. Behind them in the line, Stucki, Donovan and Schwartz huddled together for mutual protection, cowed by their first look at the dazzling show.

Al Temple was not there. He had dressed early, with care, and was waiting at the bottom of the stairs when Sheila came down in her party dress. Her attentions to him, her reading to him while he was hurt, had filled him with confidence. When she refused his arm, told him she was going with Murdock, he did not believe her. When she told him with shining eyes that she and Murdock were going to marry, he panicked, dug his fingers into her shoulders and shook her.

"No. Sheila, you can't do it. I love you too much. Come with me. We'll take that thousand dollars and get out of this rotten country. We'll go East. Now."

He tugged her toward the door but she wrenched free. She had forgotten the gold he had left with her. She dodged him and ran to the kitchen, climbed on a chair and reached for the cookie jar on the top shelf. He darted into the room behind her, saw her lift out the leather pouch and stopped beside the table, holding his breath, listening. They must get away before Murdock came downstairs.

She stepped down from the chair and came to lay the pouch on the table before him, her eyes sad on him.

"Al, Ken loves me too. And I love him. I couldn't live a lie with you."

He stood silent, his breathing shallow, reorienting himself, defeat forcing itself through to him. Very slowly he picked up the pouch, slowly dropped it into his pocket, slowly nodded. He leaned toward her and kissed her lightly, then fell back on the ancient hope of rejected suitors.

"If you ever need me . . ."

She held her misty smile for him until he had gone. Then she cried a little. She had washed her face in cold water and was waiting in the parlor when Murdock came down the stairs whistling.

As he helped her into her cloak she said softly, "Al's gone."

His tone was neutral. "He's early. But he likes a party."

"Not to the party. He's going East."

He did not risk saying anything. They waited for Stucki, met the two tunnel men in the street and walked up the hill together.

When the slow receiving line reached the host, Sutro took Murdock's hand in both of his and stepped out of his place, saying, "Come over here a minute."

He led Murdock and the girl on his arm to a small arbor, and there drew a slip of paper from his pocket, put it into Ken's fingers.

In the pink lantern glow Murdock looked at it. A check on the Nevada Bank. He stared at the amount. Eighteen thousand dollars.

"What's this?"

"For your tunnel stock."

"But there's some mistake," he said. "Ed only paid nine thousand . . ."

Sutro chuckled, beaming. "The stock is rising since the mines signed the contracts. Today it's double what your brother gave for it."

Sheila, bending to peer at the figure, tightened her hand on his arm. "Ken—Ken. We can buy the ranch back."

Murdock was without words. Before he found them, the noise of a procession of carriages turning in at the gate caught Sutro's attention.

"The President," he said, and left them, striding toward the first carriage as it stopped before the aisle of lanterns.

Sheila and Murdock watched after him, but the girl's curiosity was too much to resist.

153

"It's Grant. Come on." Her voice was breathless and she towed him forward.

He hung back, saying uncertainly, "Grant—here?"

She hauled him on. "Yes. The President and his family. They stopped off on a trip to see the Comstock. But I didn't expect them to come down here."

She wriggled through to the front of the collecting crowd. Over her head Murdock saw a blocky figure step from the carriage, the expression on his face hidden by a thick beard. After him came James Fair and then Governor Kirkland.

Sutro was shaking hands with the visitors. Sheila kept moving forward as if drawn by a magnet. It was probably the only time in her life she would have the chance to see a real live President. She did not mean to miss a detail. They came up behind Sutro, close enough to hear the President say, "I am glad to congratulate you on the completion of the tunnel. And I would like to meet some of the men who made it possible."

"Certainly, Mister President." Sutro turned, saw Murdock behind Sheila and reached out to hand them forward. "Mr. President, Ken Murdock. He is more responsible than anyone else that we have a tunnel today. He was a rancher in Oregon and I understand he means to go back there."

Murdock found himself shaking hands with Grant, Sheila still clinging to his other arm. The President glanced down and his beard twitched.

"Your wife, sir?"

"Not yet, but soon." It was all Murdock could manage to say.

Grant looked at the girl fully. "To win a wife like you he must be a very good man indeed. You might kiss him for us."

Her color came up. So did the curve of her lips. She stretched on tiptoe and kissed Murdock in front of the full crowd. Then, on the wave of the instant, she stepped to Sutro and kissed him. And that was not all. It was the only chance she would ever have. Sheila Bryan kissed the President of the United States.

John Hunter was the name used by **Todhunter Ballard** for a number of outstanding Western novels. Ballard was born in Cleveland, Ohio. He graduated with a Bachelor's degree from Wilmington College in Ohio, having majored in mechanical engineering. His early years were spent working as an engineer before he began writing fiction for the magazine market. As W. T. Ballard he was one of the regular contributors to *Black Mask Magazine* along with Dashiell Hammett and Erle Stanley Gardner. Although Ballard published his first Western story in *Cowboy Stories* in 1936, the same year he married Phoebe Dwiggins, it wasn't until *Two-Edged Vengeance* (1951) that he produced his first Western novel. Ballard later claimed that Phoebe, following their marriage, had co-written most of his fiction with him, and perhaps this explains, in part, his memorable female characters. Ballard's Golden Age as a Western author came in the 1950s and extended to the early 1970s. *Incident at Sun Mountain* (1952), *West of Quarantine* (1953), and *High Iron* (1953) are among his finest early historical titles, published by Houghton Mifflin. After numerous traditional Westerns for various publishers, Ballard returned to the historical novel in *Gold in California!* (1965) which earned him a Golden Spur Award from the Western Writers of America. It is a story set during the Gold Rush era of the 'Forty-Niners. However, an even more panoramic view of that same era is to be found in Ballard's *magnum opus, The Californian* (1971), with its contrasts between the *Californios* and the emigrant gold-seekers, and the building of a freight line to compete with Wells Fargo. It was in his historical fiction that Ballard made full use of his background in engineering combined with exhaustive historical research. However, these novels are also character-driven, gripping a reader from first page to last with their inherent drama and the spirit of adventure so true of those times.